# MURDER IN THE MEDIA

More rediscovered
serials and stories

**Francis Durbridge**

**WILLIAMS & WHITING**

Copyright © Serial Productions

This edition published in 2022 by Williams & Whiting

All rights reserved

This script is fully protected under the copyright laws of the British Commonwealth of Nations, the United States of America, and all countries of the Berne and Universal Copyright Convention. All rights including Stage, Motion Picture, Radio, Television, Public Reading and the right to translate into foreign languages are strictly reserved. No part of this publication may be lawfully reproduced in any form or by any means such as photocopying, typescript, manuscript, audio or video recording or digitally or electronically or be transmitted or stored in a retrieval system without the prior written permission of the copyright owners.

Applications for performance or other rights should be made to The Agency, 24 Pottery Lane, London W11 4LZ.

Cover design by Timo Schroeder

9781912582709

Williams & Whiting (Publishers)

15 Chestnut Grove, Hurstpierpoint,

West Sussex, BN6 9SS

Titles by Francis Durbridge published by Williams & Whiting
1   The Scarf – tv serial
2   Paul Temple and the Curzon Case – radio serial
3   La Boutique – radio serial
4   The Broken Horseshoe – tv serial
5   Three Plays for Radio Volume 1
6   Send for Paul Temple – radio serial
7   A Time of Day – tv serial
8   Death Comes to The Hibiscus – stage play
    The Essential Heart – radio play
    (writing as Nicholas Vane)
9   Send for Paul Temple – stage play
10  The Teckman Biography (tv serial)
11  Paul Temple and Steve (radio serial)
12  Twenty Minutes From Rome
13  Portrait of Alison
14  Paul Temple: Two Plays for Radio Volume 1
15  Three Plays for Radio Volume 2
16  The Other Man
17  Paul Temple and the Spencer Affair
18  Step In The Dark
19  My Friend Charles
20  A Case For Paul Temple

Murder At The Weekend – the rediscovered newspaper serials
and short stories

Also published by Williams & Whiting:
Francis Durbridge : The Complete Guide
By Melvyn Barnes

Titles by Francis Durbridge to be published by Williams &
Whiting
A Game of Murder
A Man Called Harry Brent
Bat Out of Hell
Breakaway – The Family Affair

Breakaway – The Local Affair
Melissa
Murder On The Continent (Further re-discovered serials and stories)
Paul Temple and the Alex Affair
Paul Temple and the Canterbury Case (film script)
Paul Temple and the Conrad Case
Paul Temple and the Geneva Mystery
Paul Temple and the Gilbert Case
Paul Temple and the Gregory Affair
Paul Temple and the Jonathan Mystery
Paul Temple and the Lawrence Affair
Paul Temple and the Madison Mystery
Paul Temple and the Margo Mystery
Paul Temple and the Sullivan Mystery
Paul Temple and the Vandyke Affair
Paul Temple Intervenes
The Desperate People
The Doll
One Man To Another – a novel
The World of Tim Frazer
Tim Frazer and the Salinger Affair
Tim Frazer and the Mellin Forrest Mystery
Two Paul Temple Plays for Television

# INTRODUCTION

The lengthy research leading to my book *Francis Durbridge: The Complete Guide* (Williams & Whiting, 2018) produced many fascinating discoveries. These included the fact that Francis Durbridge's first stage play was performed in Birmingham as long ago as 1943, but when in the mid-1960s he resumed his writing for the stage it was in Germany rather than the UK that his main theatrical career began. My research also revealed that Durbridge's output over many years was far more prolific and wide-ranging than was previously known, and although he usually wrote under his own name he sometimes adopted the pseudonyms Frank Cromwell, Nicholas Vane and Lewis Middleton Harvey.

Research that produces a mass of new information is both rewarding and exciting, and there was the added factor of delight when it provided the evidence to debunk many of the errors about Francis Durbridge's works that persist on the Internet. It has been acknowledged by his sons, Stephen and Nicholas, that they were previously unaware of much of what I had unearthed. They remain justifiably proud of their father's achievements and his international reputation, and have been most supportive in bringing to a modern audience the newly collected works in this book and indeed the whole series of Williams & Whiting publications. The availability in multiple volumes of the "lost" works of a single author, many decades after they were written, must be highly unusual if not unique.

But firstly, for anyone to whom Durbridge's name is unfamiliar, some background information might be helpful. Francis Henry Durbridge (1912-98) was the most popular writer of mystery thrillers for BBC radio and television from the 1930s to the 1970s, after which he enjoyed a successful career as a stage dramatist with plays such as *Suddenly at Home, Murder with Love* and *House Guest*. His radio serials have been regularly repeated in recent years, the novels based on his radio and television serials are frequently reprinted, and his stage plays remain among the staple fare of amateur and professional companies.

In the 1930s Francis Durbridge was a frequently recurring name on BBC radio, as his output included comedies and dramatic plays, children's stories, musical libretti and short sketches, but it was in 1938 that he found the niche in which he was to carve his name. His radio serial *Send for Paul Temple* became the first of a series that endured until 1968, with Paul Temple and his wife Steve established as icons of detective fiction in such serials as *Paul Temple and the Curzon Case*, *Paul Temple and the Madison Mystery*, *Paul Temple and the Vandyke Affair*, *Paul Temple and the Gilbert Case* and *Paul Temple and the Spencer Affair*. Little wonder, then, that the Paul Temple radio mysteries have long survived as books, films, CDs and DVDs, and such was his appeal that Temple even became a comic strip hero in newspapers for an incredibly long run from 1950 to 1971.

But Durbridge was also the master of the thriller serial on BBC television, undoubtedly ruling the roost for nearly thirty years – beginning with *The Broken Horseshoe* in 1952, and continuing with such titles as *Portrait of Alison*, *My Friend Charles*, *The Scarf*, *The World of Tim Frazer*, *Melissa* and *Bat out of Hell*. His complex plots and cliff-hanger endings attracted enormous viewing figures in the UK and abroad, and he changed his approach by introducing one-off protagonists rather than simply transferring Paul Temple to television.

It is therefore not surprising, given that in the 1940s and 1950s he was at his peak, that Durbridge was in demand to contribute serials and short stories to newspapers and magazines. Most of them were never reprinted after their original publication – until now. In 2020 Williams & Whiting published *Murder at the Weekend: The re-discovered serials and stories of Francis Durbridge*, containing four serials and twelve Paul Temple short stories dating from 1947 to 1959. As the title implies, they first appeared in weekend editions of their respective newspapers or magazines. And now, *Murder in the Media* continues the process of bringing Durbridge's re-discovered stories to today's readers.

The first in this volume, *Deadline for Harry*, was recorded in Durbridge's cash ledger on 20 January 1960 with a fee of £500. The recently discovered original typescript indicates that this six episode serial was written for the *News of the World*, but a search at the British Library of all 1959 and 1960 issues has failed to confirm that it was published in that newspaper. A further surprise is that Durbridge much later turned again to this plot, in connection with the 1969-71 Paul Temple television series. Although he did not himself write any of the televised episodes, he produced several synopses – including *Murder in Advance*, featuring Temple in a new version of *Deadline for Harry* (which was not adopted for television).

*Lady at the Villa*, which might be described as a novella, has an interesting history. It was originally written in 1956, and although Durbridge's ledger records on 11 January 1957 that it was bought by the *Daily Mail* there is no trace of its publication in that newspaper at the time. But many years later, under the title *The Second Chance*, a revised version masqueraded as a new Durbridge story in a one-off magazine called *The Radio Times Generation Game Christmas Special*, published by the BBC in November 1974.

Another complicated history can be seen in the magazine serial that in this volume is called *Right into the Heart*. Its first manifestation was the six-part mystery *The Man Who Beat The Panel*, which was published in the magazine *TV Mirror* from 16 April to 21 May 1955. Then seven years later it was thoroughly revised and expanded, and the new version appeared in Germany as *Mitten ins Herz* in the magazine *Bild und Funk*, in nine instalments, 1962-63. This has never until now been published in English, and Mike Linane has translated it for this first UK appearance. *Mitten ins Herz* (*Right into the Heart*) is very different from *The Man Who Beat The Panel* – although a few of the original characters appear, most of the others are re-named or entirely new and the plot is considerably amended. Today it is easy to compare it with the original serial *The Man Who Beat The Panel*, which has been published by Williams & Whiting in the above-mentioned collection *Murder at the Weekend*. And there was yet another later development, when Durbridge converted it to a Paul Temple case and wrote a synopsis called *The Elusive Miss Helvin* (intended for the 1969-71 Francis Matthews television series *Paul Temple*, but not used).

*Coffee Break* is very much a short story, but again with a history. It originally appeared as *Paul Temple and the Elstree Affair* in the *London Evening Standard* on 17 January 1947. Much later, Durbridge adapted it as *Coffee Break* which appeared in *Showguide No.6*, a London theatre programme published by Keith Prowse Ltd for Christmas 1971. And on this occasion Paul Temple was removed rather than inserted, being replaced by Detective Superintendent Hamer.

These serials and stories have been collected in book form for the very first time, and I hope they will be enjoyed by seasoned Durbridge fans as well as those who are only now becoming acquainted with his skills.

**Melvyn Barnes**
Author of *Francis Durbridge:The Complete Guide* (Williams & Whiting, 2018)

# MURDER IN THE MEDIA

| | |
|---|---|
| Deadline For Harry | 3 |
| Lady At The Villa | 39 |
| Right Into The Heart | 83 |
| Coffee Break | 199 |

2

# DEADLINE FOR HARRY

A serial story
in six episodes

## EPISODE ONE

Detective-Superintendent Max Christian was tired and faintly ill tempered. He attributed this feeling to his last job; a well-publicised and particularly sordid bigamy case.

"You look a bit under the weather, Max," said Detective-Inspector Davis, who knew Christian better than most people. "Why not take a few days off?"

"It's all right," said Christian shortly. He pushed the press clippings he had been reading into a file. The door opened and one of the duty sergeants came over to Christian.

"Does the name Peter Gibson mean anything to you, sir?" he asked.

"Should it?" snapped Christian.

"It's a young chap downstairs," explained the sergeant apologetically. "I've tried to explain to him, but he insists on seeing you. Says it's about a murder that's going to take place."

"A prophet, eh?" said Christian sourly. "I don't feel like cranks this morning, sergeant."

The sergeant looked uncomfortable. "This chap certainly doesn't look like a crank, sir."

"I'll see him if you like, Max," offered Davis.

Christian shook his head. "No, I'll see him, sergeant."

The thick-set young man in the outer office was palpably nervous. "I've been following your last case in the newspapers," he told Christian, "so when this happened, I somehow felt you were the only man who'd know what to do." He spoke softly with just a trace of Cockney accent.

3

"Let's hear a bit more about it," prompted Christian.

Peter Gibson explained that he worked in the Rio Grande coffee bar in Hampstead, which was owned by George Talbot, a well-known Hampstead businessman.

"But Mr Talbot doesn't interfere," went on Gibson, "he leaves the running of the place to me – it's quite small."

"Do you live on the premises?"

"No, I'm in digs in Swiss Cottage – 78 Redlane Gardens."

Christian made a note of the address. "Go on," he said.

"I put in long hours at the Rio Grande," continued Gibson, "but we're often slack in the afternoons. I usually have a half hour nap behind a screen in one corner – I've got an armchair there. Of course, the customers don't know I'm behind the screen; they think I'm in the kitchen."

He hesitated for a moment, and then went on: "Two days ago, the place was empty except for two casual customers – middle-aged women – having coffee. It was about a quarter to three, so I went to my chair. I read the paper for a bit and then I dozed off. I was sort of half-conscious when I suddenly heard the word 'murder' mentioned! I sat up with a jerk. Naturally, I thought for a second I'd been dreaming. Then I heard one of the women say, quite deliberately, 'The deadline is the 16th of next month. Make no mistake – they're going to kill Harry Sherwood by the 16th.'"

Christian looked at the young man for a moment before asking: "Do you often have nightmares, Mr Gibson?"

Gibson shook his head. "I tell you this was a perfectly genuine conversation, Superintendent!" He met Christian's gaze without flinching. "I'm sure they were serious. Someone is going to kill this Harry Sherwood by the 16th of next month."

"Did you know these women?"

"Never seen them before – most of our trade's casual. I've looked out for them since, but they haven't been in."

Gibson picked up one of his gloves and began to pull at the fingers with little jerks. Christian noticed that he had a nervous tic in the muscles of his left cheek.

"I'm not always as jumpy as this," the young man said quietly. "But this thing's getting me down – I haven't been able to sleep. I told George Talbot about it; I thought he might be able to suggest something."

"What did he say?"

"Told me to look it up in the dream book and said I shouldn't sleep on the job anyway."

"A natural reaction," smiled Christian. He took down a description of the two women, but beyond the fact that they were middle-aged and looked respectable, Gibson could tell him nothing about them.

"You didn't hear them say where or how this murder would take place?" he queried.

"I think they were coming to that, but they must have heard me sit up in my chair – at any rate they switched the conversation." Gibson picked up his hat. "I'm sorry if I've put you to a lot of trouble," he said. "But you've no idea what a relief it is now I've told you everything."

"That's what we're here for, Mr Gibson," said Christian. "You've left your gloves behind …"

Gibson went back for his gloves, apologised again and disappeared down the corridor.

"A bit of a nut, if you ask me," commented Davis, who had listened to the conversation.

Christian smiled. "Nevertheless, I think I'll take a half-day off tomorrow and potter around Hampstead."

Davis nodded and went out, returning almost at once with a glove he had picked up in the corridor. He handed the glove to the Superintendent. "Your friend's a bit careless with his gloves," he said.

Christian's expedition to Hampstead proved unprofitable. A newspaper seller and a postman both stated firmly that they had never heard of the Rio Grande coffee bar. He tried an estate agents' office, adding the additional information that the Rio Grande was owned by George Talbot and run by Peter Gibson. No one in the estate agents' office had heard of the Rio Grande, George Talbot, or Peter Gibson. "Believe me, sir," said the man in the office, "If this Mr George Talbot owns any property in these parts, we should certainly know him."

Twenty minutes later, Christian was ringing the bell of 78 Redlane Gardens. Through the opaque glass door panel, he could see two figures dimly outlined. The door was opened almost as once.

A gaunt looking man of about fifty stood in the doorway. He was muffled in scarf and overcoat and leaned heavily on an old-fashioned ebony walking stick. By his side stood a woman, some ten years his junior and wearing a Persian lamb coat. 'Good looker, sophisticated, hard as nails,' said Christian mentally.

Obviously, the man thought Christian was a door-to-door salesman. "Yes?" he snapped.

Christian introduced himself. "I'm Detective-Superintendent Christian from Scotland Yard," he said. "I'm looking for a man called Peter Gibson."

The woman looked at him blankly. "There's no one of that name here," she answered. "Are you sure you've got the right address?"

"Quite sure," said Christian.

"But there are only the two of us here," said the man rather querulously. "My name is Arthur Cornwallis and I'm an accountant at the Finchley Road branch of the North City Bank. This is my wife."

"You really shouldn't be standing here in the draught, Arthur," put in the woman. She turned to Christian. "He's only just recovering from influenza, you know; this is his first time out. Won't you come in?"

When the three of them were standing together in the hall, Cornwallis asked: "What's this chap Gibson been up to?"

"Nothing at all, as far as I know," answered Christian. "We're just trying to find him."

Cornwallis and his wife exchanged a quick glance. "Well, we've certainly never heard of him," said Arthur Cornwallis.


Christian and Davis sat together in the saloon bar of a public house near Scotland Yard. The Inspector said: "Either that chap Gibson's a crank, or somebody's taking us for a ride."

"There may be a bit more to it than that," said Christian. "But one thing really puzzles me – why did Gibson deliberately leave that glove behind?"

Davis looked surprised. "You can't be sure that he did," he said. "Personally, I think the whole thing's a practical joke – I reckon we've heard the end of it, Max."

Christian thoughtfully took a drink from his tankard of beer. "Do you, Fred? I'm not too sure about that ..."


Christian was turning his desk calendar to August 16th when Davis came in and put the memo in front of him. The Inspector said, in a voice of suppressed excitement: "Just in from Cranley Wood, in Hertfordshire. Murder case. They want us to take over."

Christian glanced at the memo. "What are the details?"

"The man was found in a caravan, stabbed to death." Davis looked at the Superintendent. "His name was Harry Sherwood."

Christian picked up his hat. "If anyone wants me, I'll be at Cranley Wood."

Detective-Inspector Goodward of the Hertfordshire County Police C.I.D. seemed somewhat relieved to see Christian. As they drove to the mortuary, he gave Christian the latest information on the murder.

"This caravan was parked on a farm for the weekend, in a corner of one of the fields," Goodward explained. "I'm afraid I can't tell you very much about the victim yet, except that his name's Sherwood. There was nothing of any great interest found on him."

At the mortuary, the attendant pulled the sheet back from the dead body and Christian gave a start of surprise.

"You know this man?" asked Goodward.

The Superintendent did not reply for a moment. Then he nodded. He was looking at the lifeless features of Peter Gibson.

Christian and Goodward left the mortuary together and the Superintendent asked to be taken to the caravan. On the way he told Goodward of the dead man's visit to Scotland Yard.

The police car stopped on the main road. "There's the farm," pointed Goodward. "Two hundred acres of lovely shooting country." The car turned off the main road and stopped within sight of a modern caravan. A uniformed constable stood nearby.

"Who owns the farm?" asked Christian casually as he got out of the car.

"It's owned by a friend of mine," said the Inspector. "A chap called George Talbot ..."

8

# EPISODE TWO

Christian could not repress a start of surprise when his colleague mentioned the name of George Talbot. He decided that he would like to meet Mr Talbot without delay and suggested that they should drive up to the farm immediately, leaving the inspection of the caravan until later.

"How long have you known him?" he asked Goodward.

"About three years. He sometimes asks me over for a day's shooting, and I can always rely on him for a turkey at Christmas."

They turned into the short drive leading to the farmhouse, a neat foursquare building, flanked by long prefabricated barns and milking sheds.

"Looks like a flourishing concern," remarked Christian.

"Talbot does all right," replied Goodward.

As they came to a standstill, a shooting brake backed out of the garage. The driver got out and, recognising Goodward, waved a hand in greeting.

George Talbot was a heavily built man in his late forties. His plentiful blonde hair was barely touched with grey; his complexion ruddy. There was about him an air of confidence and prosperity.

"I wondered when we'd be seeing you again, Inspector," he said. Goodward introduced Christian and the farmer led the way into the house.

As George Talbot crossed to the drinks table, he introduced his wife. Mildred Talbot was a small, plainly dressed woman with mouse coloured hair. Christian had the vague feeling that he had seen her before somewhere.

"I don't want to hear any of this nonsense about not drinking on duty," said Talbot genially. He poured generous drinks and began to talk about the murder.

"A shocking business," he said to Christian. "First time we've ever had a murder in these parts. If we can do anything to help clear it up, just say the word."

"When did you first meet this man Sherwood?" asked Christian.

"Let's see," said Talbot thoughtfully, "it must have been about six weeks ago. He came up here for milk and we got talking. Then he asked if he could put his caravan in a corner of the four-acre. We don't usually encourage that sort of thing, but he seemed a likeable sort of chap, so I said go ahead."

"Did he ever say anything about his business or profession?" Christian asked.

"Nothing much, but I had the idea that he worked for a firm of music publishers."

"Did you find the body in the caravan?"

The farmer shook his head. "Sherwood came up to the house early this morning to borrow a screwdriver. I was out, looking at a tractor half a mile away. My wife was upstairs dressing, and the maid answered the door. The girl couldn't find a screwdriver, so Mildred shouted down that she'd send one over to the caravan as soon as I got back."

He took another drink and went on: "I brought my foreman in for some coffee. We were all nattering about this tractor, so Mildred forgot to ask about the screwdriver. She remembered it during breakfast and eventually took it down to him herself. That's when she found the poor devil."

Christian turned to Mildred Talbot. "Can you remember what the time was?" he asked. He noticed that her naturally pale face had gone a shade whiter.

Her husband answered for her. "Just on half-past nine."

"Was he dead when you found him?" Christian asked.

Her eyes fluttered agitatedly. "Oh, yes – he'd been stabbed."

"Any sign of the weapon?"

She took her head with an odd jerky movement. "Everything was so untidy. The place was upside down, as if someone had been searching it."

"That's right," confirmed Goodward. "That was how we found it. But there was no trace of the weapon."

"What did you do then?" asked Christian.

Mildred Talbot said: "I ran across the fields to where George was working. He telephoned for the police." Her voice was little more than a whisper. Her husband patted her shoulder protectively. "It's all right, old girl," he said. "Finish your drink."

Christian and Goodward went down to the caravan. It was a two-berth type of the latest design and very compact. An old pre-war Morris Fourteen was attached to it and Christian made a note of its registration number.

Inside the caravan was a scene of wild disorder: two drawers under the bunks had been turned out and their contents scattered in all directions. Articles of clothing, tins of soup, magazines, sheet music, hairbrushes and shaving things, were piled in an untidy heap between the berths. There was also a photo-frame, which Christian picked up and studied closely. The photograph was of a strikingly beautiful girl with dark hair.

On one berth was a portable tape-recorder, a record player, a guitar which had obviously just been re-strung, and a pile of records in gaily coloured sleeves.

Christian left Goodward to sort through the jumble of articles on the floor and went to the door. The caravan, he noticed, was in a position of pleasant seclusion: no house was visible and it was effectively concealed from the road by a high hedge. He saw two farm workers turn into the gate at the top end of the field and begin searching the ditch. Then he heard footsteps in the grass and turned to face George Talbot.

"Any luck?" asked Talbot.

"Nothing so far, though I think you were right about his being in the music business – there's plenty of evidence of that."

"Yes, he always had the radio or the gramophone on the go."

Christian hesitated for a moment, and then asked: "Did he get any visitors?"

"Never saw any. After all, he was only here at weekends and used to go back to London Monday mornings – I think he had a flat up there."

They had just turned to enter the caravan, when a plain-clothes sergeant joined them. He was carrying a handkerchief. The sergeant opened the handkerchief and Christian found himself staring at a vicious looking knife. It had a black ivory handle and a thin, razor-sharp, polished blade.

Near the tip of the blade were two smears of blood.

Christian put the knife and portable tape-recorder in his briefcase and drove back to London. His thoughts were busy with every aspect of the murder. In particular, he wondered about Mildred Talbot. He was certain that somewhere, at some time, he had seen a striking likeness to her face.

Just opposite the Cenotaph he remembered: it was Arthur Cornwallis whom Mildred Talbot resembled.

Christian left the knife and tape-recorder at Scotland Yard and then went straight to Redlane Gardens.

Linda Cornwallis opened the door to him. "I'm afraid Arthur's out," she said. "He would go round to the bank, to let them know he'll be back at work soon." She led the way into a rather cheerless drawing room.

"I just happened to be in this area," said Christian casually, "so I thought you might like to know that we've found the man I was enquiring about."

"Oh, really?" she said disinterestedly. "I'll tell my husband. Does this man still insist that he used to lodge here?"

Christian walked over to the mantlepiece and studied a photograph intently. It was of Arthur Cornwallis as a somewhat unwilling looking Army officer.

"I'm afraid he can't insist on anything," he said quietly. "He was found murdered in a caravan near Cranley Wood."

Linda Cornwallis drew in her breath sharply. "The caravan," continued Christian evenly, "was parked on a farm belonging to a man called George Talbot."

Christian looked at her enquiringly, but she did not meet his eyes. He picked up the photograph and said: "Would Mrs Talbot be any relation of yours – or your husband's?"

She hesitated for a moment. Then she said: "Mildred Talbot is my husband's sister. But we haven't seen them for five years; Arthur and George never got on very well."

Christian indicated the photograph. "There's quite a family likeness between your husband and his sister," he remarked.

She gave a nervous little laugh. "Yes, isn't there? Most people notice it." She went on more composedly: "I must say, it's quite a coincidence that the man you were looking for should have been found on the Talbots' farm."

"Quite a coincidence," agreed Christian. "Incidentally, the Talbots knew him as Harry Sherwood. Have they ever mentioned him to you?"

Her mouth tightened. "We know nothing of the Talbots' affairs," she said coldly.

Christian garaged his car and opened the front door of his mews flat. He was just about to go into the bathroom, when he heard a slight scuffle of sound behind him.

He felt, as well as heard, the whistle of the walking stick past his right ear. Fortunately, he side-stepped just in time and took the blow on his shoulder.

The intruder came at Christian again, this time aiming a vicious kick at the Superintendent's stomach. Christian took the point of the man's shoe just below the knee-cap. As he stumbled forward, the stick came down with murderous force.

It was ten minutes before Christian recovered consciousness; then, feeling dazed and sick, he staggered into the bathroom and plunged his head into cold water.

He had just finished drying his head when the telephone rang. Lifting the receiver, he was in time to hear the click of falling coins. A woman's voice said: "Is that Superintendent Christian?"

"Christian speaking. Who's that?"

The woman said, tensely: "Try the glove on him, Superintendent. It's most important." Before Christian could reply the receiver was replaced.

For a few seconds Christian stared at the telephone in astonishment. Then suddenly he remembered. The glove that Harry Sherwood, alias Peter Gibson, had left behind was still in the drawer of his desk at Scotland Yard ...

Max Christian took the glove out of the drawer and examined it carefully, turning it inside out. There seemed to be nothing unusual about it, but he felt sure that this was what the intruder had been looking for. He could think of no other reason for the visit to his flat.

His head was throbbing slightly and there was an ache in his shoulder; nevertheless, he made up his mind to return to Cranley Wood.

The mortuary attendant seemed surprised when the Superintendent asked to see the body of Harry Sherwood again. He watched with morbid interest as Christian took a glove from his pocket and tried to pull it over the rigid left hand.

The glove was at least two sizes too small ...

# EPISODE THREE

Christian made a final attempt to fit the glove on the dead man's hand, but it was obviously too small.

The mortuary attendant was eyeing him with curiosity. "Looks like it's the wrong glove," the man ventured.

Without offering the attendant any explanation, Christian returned to his car and drove to Grangetree Farm. He was determined to see George Talbot again.

A pleasant looking girl showed the Superintendent into the hall and explained that 'the Master' was out in one of the sheds repairing a milking machine.

Left by himself, Christian glanced round the hall. On the ornate Monks' bench, he noticed a pair of gloves. He cautiously took the dead man's glove out of his pocket and compared it for size with one of the gloves on the bench. The gloves were of exactly the same quality and of identical size.

Three minutes later, George Talbot breezed in, with a cheery welcome for Christian. He led the way into the drawing room, where his wife sat sewing. She looked up apprehensively as the two men entered.

George Talbot made straight for the drinks table, but Christian refused a drink. "I won't keep you long," he said. "I just thought there were one or two facts that might interest you."

George Talbot mixed himself a generous whisky and soda but offered no comment.

Christian took the glove from his pocket and handed it to Talbot. "Do you recognise this?" he asked.

Talbot examined the glove closely. "I wouldn't swear to it," he said slowly, "but it's very like one of a pair that I once saw Sherwood wearing. Where did you find it?"

16

"Sherwood came to see me at Scotland Yard some weeks ago. He left this glove behind."

Christian went on to outline the details of that visit. He noticed that George Talbot seemed intensely interested in the story.

"Are you sure that this man who called himself Peter Gibson was really Sherwood?" asked Talbot.

"No doubt about that. However, there's one thing that I haven't told you. Gibson – or rather Sherwood – said he was employed at the Rio Grande Coffee Bar in Hampstead. He further stated that the Rio Grande was owned by," – Christian paused for effect – "a man named George Talbot."

Mildred Talbot gave a little gasp, but her husband seemed quite unconcerned. "No need to look at me like that, Super," he said jocularly. "I haven't a clue what this is about. I hate these arty characters in Hampstead and their fancy coffee bars, I wouldn't be seen dead in one, let alone own one."

"I suppose George Talbot's a fairly common name," suggested Mildred Talbot tentatively.

Christian said: "Yes, but there's still another coincidence to be explained: Gibson told me that he was lodging at 78 Redlane Gardens."

This time the effect on both the Talbots was instantaneous: George Talbot coughed in the act of drinking and his wife's hand flew to her throat.

"You know that address?" asked Christian.

Talbot quickly recovered his composure. "Yes, of course. It's where that namby-pamby brother of my wife's lives, damn his cotton spats! But Arthur can't be involved in this; he wouldn't have the guts to murder a tame flea!"

"They deny that Harry Sherwood, alias Peter Gibson, was living there," said Christian.

"Then you've seen my brother?" asked Mrs Talbot.

Christian nodded. "His wife told me they don't see much of you."

"Haven't laid eye on 'em for five years or more," declared Talbot forcibly. "And I haven't shed any tears on that account, I can tell you. Fact is, Super, we don't like them and they don't like us."

George Talbot, concluded Christian, seemed genuinely baffled by the appearance of Arthur Cornwallis in the case. He pressed Christian to stay and discuss it further, but the Superintendent told him he was due back at Scotland Yard.


It was nearly nine o'clock when Christian swung out of the drive into the lane. Suddenly, a car shot past and, recognising the driver, Christian instinctively followed it. The car turned into the narrow cart track leading to the field where the caravan was parked.

Christian left his car on the grass verge and followed the other on foot. He found it parked near the gate leading out of the field.

The moon had risen and, standing behind a hawthorn bush, Christian could just see the vague outline of the caravan. He was prepared for a fairly long wait, but after about five minutes, he heard the field gate open. He peered round the bush and saw the figure of a woman walking towards the car.

When she was ten yards away, the moonlight was strong enough to outline her features. It was Linda Cornwallis.

As she passed him, Christian noticed that she was holding her right arm against her coat, as if she had a parcel underneath. He watched her until she got into the car and drove away. Then he went over to the caravan. The door was locked.

Christian walked thoughtfully back to his car. He wondered how Linda Cornwallis had secured a key to the caravan and what she had been so anxious to find there.

Back at Cranley Wood Police Station, Christian asked the sergeant if he could see Harry Sherwood's possessions. Amongst them he found a bunch of keys. He signed a receipt for the keys and borrowed a torch from the sergeant. Just before he went, the sergeant said: "There was a message from the Yard for you to ring Inspector Davis, sir."

Davis sounded pessimistic when Christian telephoned him. "We had a report from Fingerprints," he said. "There's nothing on the knife. Incidentally, that's a wire recorder of Sherwood's. Continental, battery type."

"Have you played it?"

"Yes, the wire's clean – nothing on it."

"We're going no place fast!" said Christian. "See you later, Fred."

Christian drove back to the caravan. He parked his car under a tree, where Mrs Cornwallis had left her car an hour before. He took the torch and switched off all the lights. He stood in the field for a moment, listening intently. But there was no sound except for the shuffle of cattle in a near-by field.

Christian found a key that fitted the door of the caravan. He closed it after him and switched on the torch, keeping the beam well below the level of the windows.

At first glance nothing seemed to have been disturbed. The record player, guitar, and radio were in the same places. The pile of records was still there …

The torch beam stayed on the records for a few seconds. Christian had the feeling that they had been disturbed: he recalled that the top record had been selections from 'My Fair Lady', in its attractive sleeve. The uppermost sleeve now had an unmistakably middle-west look about it – it was 'Oklahoma'. Clearly, someone had been looking through the records.

Christian picked up the top sleeve; it was empty. It took him only a few seconds to discover that all the records had been taken from their sleeves.

Christian completed his inspection of the caravan's interior, then picked up the empty record sleeves and left. A low mist had settled about two feet above ground level and the night was now distinctly chilly.

When he reached his car again, it seemed to be floating on a sea of mist, with the wheels completely hidden. He opened the driver's door and pushed the record sleeves into the compartment under the dashboard.

Suddenly, the extraordinary feeling possessed Christian that there was someone in the car – there was just a faint hint of perfume.

Gripping the steering wheel with his right hand, he realised that he presented a perfect target to anyone in the back of the car. Holding the torch at arm's length, he flashed the light on the back seat.

A woman's body was slumped in the far corner, the face obscured by the upholstery. A headscarf had been twisted tightly round her neck.

Christian opened the back door of the car and turned the woman's face towards him.

The powerful beam from the torch threw into grotesque relief the distorted features of Mildred Talbot ...

# EPISODE FOUR

It needed only a brief examination of the body to tell Christian that Mildred Talbot was dead. He carefully locked the car and turned towards the main road. It was still bright moonlight as he walked up the drive to Grangetree Farm.

George Talbot seemed badly shaken when Christian broke the news of his wife's death. The colour drained from his features as he collapsed into the nearest chair.

He raised a bewildered face to Christian. "But how could it have happened?" he asked hoarsely. "It's less than half an hour since she went to see Miss Dowling."

"Who's Miss Dowling?"

"A friend of hers in the village. She rang up about an hour ago, saying she'd been taken ill."

Christian asked: "Did you hear your wife talking to Miss Dowling?"

"No, I was upstairs at the time. I heard the phone ring. When I came down, Mildred said she had to see Miss Dowling right away."

"Then why should she have gone down the cart track to the caravan?"

Talbot rubbed his forehead in bewilderment. "I've no idea. She could have been carried down there, I suppose – and then dumped in your car."

The Superintendent nodded. "That's a possibility."

Christian telephoned Inspector Goodward at Cranley Wood and gave him brief details of the murder. Then he visited Miss Dowling. The old lady was apparently in normal health and had not used the telephone that evening.

Although he did not get home until well after midnight, Christian was at his desk at nine o'clock the next morning. The file on the Sherwood case was in front of him.

He briefly outlined the events of the previous evening to Inspector Davis. Davis asked: "Have you any idea who phoned Mildred Talbot?"

"I don't even know for certain that there was a call. I've only Talbot's word for it."

"Has anything else come in about Sherwood? Or the girl whose photograph was in the caravan?"

Christian shook his head.

Davis said: "What about this Cornwallis woman? Why was she prowling around?"

"She was after some gramophone records." Christian indicated the small pile of empty record sleeves on his desk.

"Could this strangling job have been done by a woman?" hazarded Davis.

"Definitely not. It was done by a man – and a strong man at that."

Christian turned to the file again. "I've had an interesting report from Roberts," he said. "He's been making some enquiries from the Bank about Arthur Cornwallis."

"Isn't he a pillar of respectability?"

Christian glanced at the report sheet. "He was transferred to Finchley Road about the beginning of July, before that he was at the Leyton Green branch."

Davis looked up sharply. "Leyton Green? That was the branch where they had a big robbery about three months ago."

"That's it," said Christian. "They got away with ninety-five thousand pounds. Not a penny has been recovered, nor a man traced. It was the Bank job of the year."

Davis looked at Christian. "This is an interesting coincidence."

Max Christian nodded. "It is indeed," he said quietly.

Christian had to ring three times before Arthur Cornwallis opened the door. Cornwallis looked pale and strained; he stared apprehensively at the sergeant who accompanied the Superintendent. He pulled the scarf he was wearing more closely round his throat and ushered them into the inhospitable drawing room.

Christian stood with his back to the fireplace. "Perhaps I could have a word with your wife," he said.

"I'm afraid she's not here," said Cornwallis. "She left early this morning to visit some relatives in Manchester. Is there anything I can do?"

"I'm afraid there's some bad news about your sister," said Christian.

"I know," said Cornwallis in a lifeless voice, "her husband telephoned. A shocking business, Superintendent."

"I suppose you can't suggest who might want to murder Mrs Talbot?"

"I'm afraid I know very little about her affairs," replied Cornwallis. "You see, we never visited them."

"What would you say," continued Christian deliberately, "if I told you that your wife was seen in Cranley Wood last night, shortly before your sister was murdered?"

"But that's ridiculous," protested Cornwallis. "She was at her bridge club all the evening."

"How do you know that?"

"Because she told me – she goes there every Wednesday."

Christian read out the number of the car he had seen Linda Cornwallis enter the previous evening. "Is that your car, sir?" he asked.

Cornwallis swallowed. "Yes," he said, "that's the number of my car. What – what are you going to do?"

"Search this house," said Christian quietly, producing a document from his inside pocket.

Cornwallis stared at the search warrant and shrugged resignedly. "Very well," he said. "But I've really no idea what you expect to find."

It took less than five minutes to find the small pile of records beside a portable record player.

Christian checked the titles with a list in his pocket. Arthur Cornwallis seemed completely mystified by the entire proceedings.

At Scotland Yard, the fingerprints on the records were checked with those on the sleeves. There were two sets: presumably those of the murdered man and Linda Cornwallis.

Christian and Davis spent the next two hours listening to the records. There was nothing in any way remarkable about any of them; they were simply recordings of current popular tunes. Christian finally sent them down to the laboratory for further tests. "Not that I've much hope of finding anything," he said to Davis.

"Then what did Mrs Cornwallis expect to find?" asked the Inspector.

Christian smiled grimly. "Whatever it was, I've an idea she was mistaken."

Davis sighed. "So where does that get us?"

"I'm not sure," said Christian. "But my guess is – back to Cranley Wood ..."

Inspector Goodward was clearly pleased to see Christian when he walked into his office. He said: "Got a bit of news for you, sir. You remember the photograph of the girl we found in the caravan?"

"Yes. What about it?"

"She was here an hour ago," explained Goodward. "She gave her name as June Sherwood – said she was the dead man's sister. Apparently, she's been working in Paris and when she read about the murder she flew over."

"You're sure she's the same girl?"

"She's the dead spit of the photograph," said Goodward emphatically.

"What did she say?"

"She seemed more concerned about the contents of the caravan than her brother's death," replied Goodward. "Of course, I told her she couldn't take anything away yet. She's booked a room at the pub just up the road – the White Hart."

"Good," said Christian. "Ring her up and ask her to meet me in the bar – say in half an hour."

June Sherwood proved to be an attractive, elaborately made-up brunette in her middle twenties. She listened in wide-eyed silence while Christian told her about her brother's murder; there was a suspicion of moisture in the grey-blue eyes.

"But haven't you any idea at all who might have killed him?" she queried. Her voice was low-pitched and attractive.

"We're still working on it," said Christian. "I'm relying on you to help us."

"Of course, I'll do anything I can," she assured him. "But I haven't seen my brother for about a year. He was out of work, and I lent him two hundred pounds. Since then, I heard in a roundabout way that he was working for a recording company."

Christian picked up their empty glasses and ordered fresh drinks at the serving hatch. When he came back, he said: "Do you know if he was married?"

"Not as far as I know." She smiled at Christian. "I'm afraid Harry and I were never the marrying sort."

Christian raised his glass. "You're still very young," he said.

"I suppose I am." Her voice suddenly hardened a little. "All the same, I'd like to get my two hundred pounds back …"

25

"I quite understand," said Christian sympathetically. "I'll fix it at the police station for you to look round the caravan. Of course, you can't strip it completely, but if there's anything there you fancy, we'll turn a blind eye."

June Sherwood looked at Christian with renewed interest. "Well," she explained, and there was provocation in her voice; "perhaps policemen are human after all ..."

Goodward regarded Christian curiously. "You mean you want her to have the key to the caravan?"

Max Christian nodded. "And that's not all. When she's clear of the caravan, bring her back here and have her searched. That girl's definitely after something – Something that belongs to her brother. I've got to know what it is, Inspector."

Goodward made a note on a pad. "Isn't this a little unorthodox, sir?" he ventured.

Christian smiled enigmatically. "I'm rather an unorthodox character," he said.

As June Sherwood left the caravan early the next morning, a plain-clothes detective picked her up.

She was carrying the guitar ...

# EPISODE FIVE

Inspector Goodward lost no time in telling Christian about June Sherwood and in sending the guitar to Scotland Yard. Christian was humming happily to himself when Davis came into his office.

"You're looking as pleased as a cat with two tails," commented Davis. "Something gone right for a change."

Christian told him the news.

"But what the devil would June Sherwood want with the guitar?" asked Davis.

"We'll know more about that when we've taken a look at it. Poor old Goddard's pretty baffled – swears there's absolutely nothing hidden inside the thing."

Christian picked up another report from the folder in front of him.

"Here's something else," he said. "I had Sherwood's fingerprints checked with the one print they found on the door of the manager's office in the Leyton Green Bank job. It's the same all right."

Davis whistled softly. "So Sherwood was concerned in the bank robbery," he mused. "And none of the money was recovered. If he hadn't been murdered, we might really be on to something."

"We're doing all right," Christian assured him. "It's my belief that the money has never come into circulation and that Sherwood had it hidden away somewhere – hence the murder. He was given until the $16^{th}$ to hand it over – or else! He was sticking out for a bigger cut, but his friends warned him that if he started spending the money, they'd tip off the police."

Davis frowned thoughtfully. "Then what was the idea of Sherwood coming here and pitching us that yarn about the murder?"

"He was keeping up his bluff to the last minute," explained Christian. "He wanted to make sure that if his pals carried out their threat and killed him, the police would have several clues. So he spun us that yarn about the women in the coffee bar, knowing that if he was murdered we'd follow up the names he'd mentioned."

"And if there were no murder, then the whole thing would be forgotten," reflected Davis.

"Exactly. There'd be nothing to investigate."

"D'you think he left that glove behind deliberately?"

Christian nodded. "That was to throw even more suspicion on to Talbot."

"Then who phoned you about the glove?"

"My guess is Mildred Talbot. Anyhow, the chap who searched my flat was obviously looking for that glove."

Davis lit a cigarette. "It's beginning to add up," he admitted. "We had one or two tip-offs that the boys who did the Bank job had fallen out amongst themselves. They were obviously terrified of each other, or of the boss. Looks as if they had good reason to be, judging by what happened to Sherwood."

Christian walked over to the window and watched a tug towing a string of barges down river.

"Sherwood tried to get a message to his sister, so that she could collect the loot," he said. "He's hidden it somewhere or other. The rest of the gang have tried to find that message. That explains what Mrs Cornwallis was up to – she thought the message might be on one of the gramophone records."

"It would have been easier to make a tape recording," observed Davis. "Don't forget he had a portable recorder in the caravan."

Christian stared at the Inspector, then suddenly walked round the desk and took hold of his arm. "Fred!" he

28

exclaimed. "I've got it! Now I know why that girl wanted the guitar."

Five minutes later, Christian was holding the instrument and pointing to the guitar strings. "Look at these strings," he said. "They're not nylon, they're wire – and very fine wire at that!"

"You mean it's recording wire?"

"That's exactly what I mean!"

"Good God," explained Davis. "I wouldn't have spotted that in a thousand years. I'd have just taken the guitar for granted!"

Christian smiled. "Ask Sergeant Bryce to bring Sherwood's recorder up here," he said.

Sergeant Bryce removed the wire from the guitar and skilfully threaded it into the portable recorder. Then the three men sat back and listened to the message, spoken in the familiar voice of Harry Sherwood and addressed to his sister. Christian had it played through again, jotting down the important points on his pad. Finally, he turned to the sergeant.

"I want this recorder returned to the caravan," he said. He looked at Davis for a few moments, deep in thought.

"Fred, who's that chap in the Filing Department that does impersonations?"

"You mean Sergeant Harrison? I heard a rumour he was turning professional and leaving the force."

"We've got a job for him before he goes," said Christian. "Have him come up here right away ..."

Christian and June Sherwood sat together in the small residents' lounge of the White Hart. She was pale, Christian noticed, and clearly prepared to be uncooperative.

"I don't like your methods, Superintendent," she said. Her tone was sulky and antagonistic.

"I'm trying to find out who killed your brother, Miss Sherwood," he reminded her. "My methods are no concern of yours."

"I don't see what you hoped to prove by taking that guitar," she said petulantly.

"It's helped to prove at least two things," returned Christian. "Firstly, that you and your brother were involved in the Bank robbery; secondly, it seems highly probable that you were associated with his murderer."

"But I had nothing to do with the robbery or the murder!" she protested. "You must believe that."

"Then why were you interested in the guitar? Did you know about the message?"

She nodded. "Harry told me about the robbery. When he borrowed two hundred pounds from me, he said he hoped to be able to repay it soon. Then there was trouble; they tried to make him hand over all the money. He suspected that they were going to double-cross him, or even kill him, so he took the money away and hid it. He told me that if anything happened to him, the strings of the guitar would reveal the hiding place. That's all I know."

Christian digested this thoughtfully. "How many other people knew about this?" he asked.

"Not another soul," she said positively. She leaned forward in her chair and Christian could see that her lower lip was trembling. "I know Harry went off the rails, but – well, I'm not a crook, Superintendent – whatever you may think."

Christian looked at her keenly for a moment. "Are you really anxious to have your brother's murderer arrested?"

She nodded vehemently. "Of course."

"Then there's something you can do to help," said Christian quickly. "It might just tip the scale in our favour …"

Early the next morning, a taxi stopped at the front door of Grangetree Farm and June Sherwood got out, carrying the guitar. George Talbot seemed to have been expecting her, for he opened the front door almost as soon as she rang.

"You just caught me when you phoned," he said. "I was going out for the day." He led the way into the drawing room.

"What can I do for you, Miss Sherwood?"

"I wondered how well you knew my brother," said June hesitantly. "You see, we hardly set eyes on each other for years, and I know nothing about his friends."

George Talbot shrugged. "I'm afraid I can't tell you much," he said. "He was only here for a few weeks."

She indicated the guitar. "Did he ever say anything to you about this guitar?"

"No, I don't think so. How did you come by it?"

"The police loaned it to me. Harry said it was worth a lot of money, but there doesn't seem to be anything particularly valuable about it."

Talbot rubbed his chin thoughtfully. "I can't say I've ever heard of a guitar being worth a large sum of money," he said. "Didn't your brother give you any clue as to why it might be valuable?"

June Sherwood shook her head. "He said something about a message and the strings of the guitar, but I don't honestly know what he was talking about."

Talbot contemplated the instrument for a moment. "On second thoughts," he said, "there is something I can do. A friend of mine keeps a music shop – I could ask him to take a look at it."

June put the guitar down on the arm of the settee. "I'd be very grateful if you would show it to your friend. When can you let me know about it? I'll be at the White Hart for the next day or two."

"I'll phone you there tomorrow morning," promised Talbot.

Immediately June Sherwood left the farm, Talbot went down to the caravan. It took him five minutes to find the recorder.

Half an hour later he was listening to an excellent impersonation by Detective-Sergeant Harrison of the voice of Harry Sherwood.

# EPISODE SIX

George Talbot switched off the recorder and returned to the caravan. He picked up the photograph of June Sherwood, carefully removed the back of the frame, and extracted a small ticket.

It was a left luggage ticket issued at Victoria Station.

An hour later, Talbot was driving his car in the direction of London. He left the car at a garage and walked to the station.

A quick glance at the Continental departures board told him that the Golden Arrow was due to leave in twenty minutes. He booked a ticket to Paris and strolled over to the left luggage office. After a momentary hesitation, he proffered the ticket and stood, nervously drumming his fingers on the counter, as the clerk searched for the luggage. Talbot was visibly relieved when the man reappeared, carrying a bulky suitcase.

Talbot settled himself in the empty compartment that accommodated four people and opened his newspaper. The headline 'Caravan murder – Early arrest expected' immediately caught his eye. Before he could read the news story, the door of the compartment slid open. Talbot looked up to see Superintendent Christian and a heavily built detective-sergeant standing over him.

Talbot's hand flew to his overcoat pocket and came out holding a small automatic pistol. The automatic pointed unwaveringly at Christian's stomach.

"I shouldn't, if I were you," advised Christian. "You'll only make it worse for yourself."

There was an ugly glint in Talbot's eyes. His finger tightened on the trigger. Then suddenly, the train gave an unexpected jolt. Moving extraordinarily quickly for a man of his bulk, the sergeant made a dive for Talbot's pistol hand, simultaneously throwing a smashing right-handed punch to the point of his jaw. The gun dropped to the floor and Talbot collapsed into his seat.

"I can see you're still after that heavyweight championship," remarked Christian. "But you really shouldn't have done that, sergeant."

The sergeant turned an aggrieved face to Christian. "What was I supposed to do, sir?" he asked. "Let him shoot you?"

"It's an interesting point," said the Superintendent drily. "Bring it up again some time."

A few minutes later, Talbot groaned and sat up. He glared at the two police officers and gingerly nursed his jaw.

Christian sat next to Talbot, and after issuing the official caution he said: "You may as well tell us the whole story, Talbot."

Talbot said, softly, "So this was a trap?"

"If you mean was that message on the wire faked, and the ticket planted, then the answer is 'yes'," replied Christian. He pointed to the suitcase. "Incidentally, that's packed with old newspapers, so you needn't bother to open it."

Talbot made a choking noise. The sergeant regarded him dispassionately and continued to write in his notebook. After a moment, Talbot said: "What else d'you know?"

"We know where the real stuff was buried," said Christian levelly. "In a neat little hole right under the caravan."

Talbot suddenly seemed to crumple. "The swine!" he muttered, "I –"

"Look," interrupted Christian, "don't be a damn fool all your life. We know who's really behind all this, so why should you carry the can?"

Talbot hesitated, then said: "Arthur Cornwallis got all the inside information, of course, and the impressions of the keys.

Sherwood was just the look-out man and general dogsbody." He hesitated a moment. "We thought we were being pretty clever, letting him hold the stuff until it wasn't hot any longer – we'd promised him a ten per cent cut. Sherwood double-crossed us and stuck out for a fifty-fifty split. Then we heard that he'd gone to Scotland Yard –"

"So, you knifed him," interposed Christian.

"I was acting on orders! We had to get rid of him!"

"Did you have to kill your wife, too?"

Talbot turned away from Christian and looked out of the window. "She'd found out about the robbery and threatened to tell the police," he said. "I was scared stiff she was going to blurt out something when you called that evening. She knew too much so she – she had to go. I was taking the body to some woods near-by when I saw your car; I hadn't realised you were still snooping around. I dumped the body in your car and beat it back to the farm." Talbot faced the Superintendent again; a note of defiance in his voice. "What the hell else d'you want to know?"

Christian leaned back and folded his arms. "What made Sherwood park his caravan in one of your fields? I should have thought he'd have given you a wide berth."

"He was after his fifty per cent; thought he could get me on his side and the deal would go through without any hard feelings" – Talbot drew a deep breath – "Are you sure he had the stuff hidden under the caravan? I used to nose around there quite a bit, but I never found any sign of digging."

"Sherwood covered it up very nicely," said Christian, "he even replaced the turf. But you can take my word for it – we found every pound that was stolen."

Max Christian climbed the gangway of 'The Maid of Orleans' and, after a brief word with the Captain, strolled down to one of the private cabins. He signalled to a plain-clothes sergeant to join him as he tapped on the cabin door.

A woman's voice called: "Yes? What is it?" Christian pushed the door open.

The good-looking woman, busy with a lipstick in front of the mirror, did not turn round. Christian realised that she was watching him carefully in the mirror. He closed the door behind him.

"I'm afraid I shall have to ask you to come ashore with me, Mrs Cornwallis," he said. She acknowledged his presence by the merest lift of the shoulders.

"I hope you have the necessary authority, Superintendent," she said frigidly.

"You hope I haven't," he corrected. "I'm afraid the game's up. We arrested your husband this morning and we've just taken George Talbot into custody. He's told us all we want to know."

She turned to face him. "What are you trying to tell me?" she asked slowly.

"That Talbot has confessed to both murders and to being involved in the Bank robbery. Also, that he was acting under instructions – instructions from you, Mrs Cornwallis."

She slowly screwed the cap on to her lipstick and replaced it in her handbag.

"Do you really think you can prove those charges?" she asked unemotionally.

"I think we can," said Christian. He stood looking at her for a moment with a kind of unwilling admiration.

"You were the brains behind the whole affair," he said. "You twisted Talbot round your little finger and the same goes for your husband – you never gave the poor devil any peace until he'd supplied all the information you wanted about the Bank. Then you roped in young Sherwood to do as much of the dirty work as possible. Well, am I right?"

She did not answer. Christian noticed that her eyes were roving casually round the cabin, as if looking for some means of escape. There was none, apart from the cabin door. Christian looked at his watch.

"The boat is due to sail in five minutes," he said.

With a hint of a sigh, she rose to her feet.

"The steward will bring your suitcase," said Christian.

She nodded and picked up her crocodile handbag.

When they reached the turn in the corridor, Linda Cornwallis suddenly stopped. "My gloves!" she exclaimed. "I've left my gloves in the cabin." She turned towards him and forced a smile. "May I go back for them, Superintendent?"

Christian hesitated, then took the handbag from under her left arm. He opened the bag, examined the contents, and finally took out a small plastic container that held a single green capsule. He knew instantly that the capsule was lethal. Christian looked at her for a moment; her lips were trembling slightly, and she was no longer smiling. Finally, he put the capsule in his overcoat pocket and returned her handbag to her. "Yes, you can go back and get your gloves," he said. "Why not?"

It was Max Christian's turn to smile.

# THE END

# LADY AT THE VILLA

A serial story

in nine episodes

## EPISODE ONE

As he drove his smart blue Lancia up the winding road that leads from Portofino Harbour into the villa-studded hills above, Dr Ricola's thoughts were far away. He was remembering another occasion when he had been urgently summoned to the Villa Serena, the summer residence where Mrs Sanderstead spent three or four months every year.

It was odd, he reflected, that he still thought of her as Mrs Sanderstead, though her first husband had died some six years ago, and she had married again. Perhaps it was because she and her first husband had made such a vivid impression on him the first time he had been invited to dine at the villa.

Lewis Sanderstead had been quiet and reserved, so different from the doctor's preconceived notion of a rich American oil baron; his beautiful young wife was utterly charming with her faint Southern accent. It had been a shock to Ricola's hopes when, shortly after Lewis Sanderstead's death, she abruptly disappeared from Portofino. He had been able to help her a great deal during the early days of her bereavement and he had begun to wonder if the friendship which had been forged at the time of stress might ripen into something more.

For four years, the Villa stood empty though everyone in Portofino knew that it still belonged to Mrs Sanderstead.

Each spring, Ricola found himself wondering whether she would return. But when at last she did, it was with a new husband, Larry Conway.

Almost as soon as she was back at the Villa, Rita invited Ricola to dinner. He went expecting to dislike the new husband. Yet he could not help being attracted by Larry Conway's gay buccaneerish personality. In the doctor's eyes, he had one great merit; he had succeeded in making Rita radiantly happy – perhaps happier than she had ever been before.

Yet there was something unfathomable and mysterious about Conway. His background was undefined, and he never spoke of the life he had led before Rita brought him to Portofino. If Ricola had a fault it was his inquisitiveness. Yet after half-a-dozen social visits to the Villa, he had still been unable to discover the circumstances under which Rita had met Larry.

"*È curioso,*" he murmured to himself as he slowed for the gates to the Villa. "Most couples will tell you a dozen times how they first met. But these two are like a pair of conspirators.

Larry Conway's formative years had been occupied by the war. After several years of intense excitement and danger he had been unable to adapt himself to any settled job. He had become a wanderer, drifting from country to country and living on his wits.

He soon discovered a flair for gambling and found that it paid him to frequent the most fashionable resorts and stay at the best hotels. Though a true soldier of fortune he was never a cheat. If he prospered, it was simply because his wits were sharper than those who pitted themselves against him.

It was not surprising that when the *Queen of Orleans*, a sumptuous vessel carrying four hundred wealthy passengers on a world cruise, dropped anchor for three days in the Venice

Lagoon, Larry Conway was staying at the Grand Palace Hotel out on the Lido. Coincidence did take a hand at one point however, for Mrs Sanderstead had decided to leave the ship for three days during the visit to Venice. The suite occupied by Larry was reserved for her from the Tuesday of that week.

Rita Sanderstead arrived early on the Tuesday morning. Larry had not even begun to pack his luggage when the hotel manager came running up to his room to tell him that Mrs Sanderstead had arrived. He must vacate the room immediately.

"But I'm entitled to use this room till midday," Larry objected. "Who is this Mrs Sanderstead that everyone is making such a fuss about?"

"She is the widow of Lewis Sanderstead," the manager said with dignity. "So please be as quick as you can, sir."

Even Larry was impressed by this information. Peeping from his balcony he caught a glimpse of Rita Sanderstead reclining gracefully on a chair on the terrace below.

When fifteen minutes later the manager led Mrs Sanderstead up to Larry's room, he found the Englishman lying on the bed groaning, his brow beaded with sweat.

"It's a fever I picked up in the tropics," he murmured weakly in answer to the manager's questions. "Be all right in a day or two. Just bring me plenty of iced water."

He heard the hapless voice of the manager as he explained to an impatient Mrs Sanderstead that something would be done, an ambulance would be sent for, the police summoned.

"No." Rita Sanderstead had made up her mind with typical promptness. "If the poor man is ill, he'd better be left in peace. I can quite as well stay on the *Queen of Orleans*."

Larry made a recovery so rapid as to be almost miraculous.

The *Queen of Orleans* next port of call was Naples. Independent as ever, Rita Sanderstead spurned the conducted tour of Pompeii and set out by herself to explore the picturesque streets of the poor quarter of Naples. She had been walking for about half an hour, when she found herself trapped in a blind alley, her way of escape barred by an unusually persistent band of street beggars. They pressed so close around her that it almost seemed as if there was some more sinister purpose in their attentions.

Suddenly, she became aware that the crowd was melting away. A tall man, who still gave the impression of youth, though he was in his middle thirties, was dispersing the crowd in succinct Italian. When the last beggar had fled, he addressed her in English.

"No harm done?"

Rita smiled at him. "I was beginning to wonder if it was a deliberate plot to kidnap me."

She saw his amused glance travel over her expensive clothes, her jewels and crocodile-skin handbag.

"I have a car just round the corner. May I drive you back to your hotel?"

"As a matter of fact," Rita said, "I'm not staying in a hotel. I'm on a ship – the *Queen of Orleans*."

Larry Conway checked in his stride and looked down at her. His face expressed surprise.

"That's a coincidence. I owe a very great debt to one of your fellow passengers – a Mrs Sanderstead."

Laughing, Rita explained who she was. Larry's evident astonishment and appreciation of her kindness delighted her. He insisted on taking her to lunch and she in turn invited him to dine on the ship that night.

When they parted at the gangway late in the afternoon, the handclasp they exchanged was held for a significant extra moment. As Larry turned away, he almost bumped into a tall, distinguished-looking man carrying a Panama hat. He had been politely waiting for Rita and Larry to finish their goodbyes.

During the days that the ship was in Naples, Rita met Larry constantly. That she was rich and beautiful he already knew. He was discovering with delight that she had also a most attractive personality. A wonderful vision was beginning to open up before him.

He took her to Pompeii, Castellammare and several times to Sorrento, so beloved of Italian sweethearts and honeymooners.

When the ship sailed, Rita's eyes were moist with unshed tears.

"Take a look towards Sorrento as the ship sails out," Larry said. "I shall be sitting at our favourite café."

An hour later, Larry sat smoking at a café table, watching the imposing bulk of the *Queen of Orleans* steaming out over water glittering in a golden sunset. He had taken a gamble and now he was waiting to see if it would come off.

He ground a half-smoked cigarette and felt in his pocket for a fresh one. From behind his chair, a slim, cold hand was placed over his eyes and a lighted cigarette put between his lips. Larry recognised the distinctive taste of Rita's lipstick. "Welcome home, darling," he said quietly.

The *Queen of Orleans* sailed on.

Two weeks later Rita and Larry were married.

Dr Ricola accelerated through the gates to the Villa Serena and up the winding avenue. Rita had said: "Hurry. It's urgent!" The same words she had used the night when Lewis Sanderstead lay writhing on his bed with acute pains in the stomach.

Though he had never said so, Dr Ricola had suspected poisoning at the time. Now he had been sent for again. Larry Conway was suffering from exactly the same symptoms.

43

# EPISODE TWO

An anxious Rita led the doctor to the long ground-floor sitting room at the Villa Serena. Larry was stretched out on the couch and this time the beads of sweat on his brow were genuine.

"It is the third time I've had this, Doctor. I didn't think it was worth bothering you, but this bout really had me doubled up."

"Well, let's have a look at you." The doctor bent and began to probe Larry's bared torso with expert hands. He half-turned towards Rita. "Do you think he could have eaten anything that disagreed with him?"

"Did you eat anything in Santa Margherita, darling? You remember you'd been down there each of the other times you had this pain."

"No. All I had was a gin and Italian at Romano's."

"I warned you not to drink Italian gin, darling," Rita protested. "Why didn't you stick to Carpano or Campari Bitter?"

Ricola was reassuring as he straightened up. He prescribed a sedative and instructed Larry to take no food other than a glass of hot milk before teatime.

"I'll come and take another look at you in the morning. Meantime, bed's the best place for you."

Rita took the doctor aside and led him out onto the terrace. It commanded one of the finest views on the west coast of Italy. She rang for drinks and a well-laden trolley was pushed out onto the terrace by Maddalena, the Italian maid who had served Rita ever since she first bought the Villa

Serena. She smiled respectfully in answer to the doctor's nod of recognition and melted away into the house.

"Tell me frankly, Mario," said Rita in a low voice. "Is Larry really all right? You're not concealing anything, are you?"

"It's difficult to say at this stage," Ricola hedged. "But I find no cause for alarm." He sipped his drink and then added quietly, "But it's rather curious, isn't it? Your first husband had very much the same complaint, didn't he?"

Rita's face hardened and she seemed to withdraw into herself. Now that the subject was broached, Ricola persisted.

"Rita, you asked me to be frank. I might say the same thing to you. You've never told me the true cause of Lewis's death. What did he die of?"

Rita turned a shoulder towards him and busied herself with lighting a cigarette from the cocktail trolley. She was saved from answering by the appearance of Larry at the French windows of the sitting room.

"Darling, you know you shouldn't be up." She moved anxiously towards him and Ricola frowned with impatience. His chance was gone, and he knew Rita would not let him return to the subject. He took his leave and left Larry and Rita alone.

"I couldn't help hearing what Mario said to you, Rita. You know, you are rather secretive about Lewis. I hardly know anything about him."

"If it comes to that, you haven't told me very much about yourself, darling. At least, not about your life before I met you."

Larry felt the cat rubbing against his legs. It was a visitor from one of the neighbouring villas and they had named it Troilus because it always seemed to be in search of a vanished lady-friend.

"Oh, I was a prize cad," Larry answered lightly. "I didn't do an honest day's work in my life, and I made my living by sponging on honest folk."

Rita seemed amused. Suddenly serious, Larry stood in front of her and lifted her chin, forcing her to meet his eyes. He knew that even though he had wooed her for all the wrong reasons, he could not bear now to live without her. "If that were really true, would it make a great difference to you?"

For answer, Rita took a cigarette from the box, lit it and placed it between his lips. It bore the faintest tang of lipstick and once again he was carried back to the moment in Sorrento that had changed his whole life.

Larry was hungry before bedtime, but he obeyed Ricola's instructions and obediently limited himself to a glass of hot milk. Next morning, he felt much better, and Ricola did not even feel it necessary to examine him when he called.

Rita had an appointment with her hairdresser that afternoon. Larry went down to Santa Margherita with her in her car. He whiled away the time by visiting his regular haunt in the little port – the small modern bar known as Romano's. As soon as he went in, the waiter began to mix him the usual cocktail, but Larry wagged his forefinger in the Italian gesture of refusal.

"I'm on the wagon today, Carlo. Make it an *aranciata.*"

Carlo made a mock serious expression as he poured the orange juice.

"This is very grave, Mr Conway. It is true then what Maddalena tells me – that you have been unwell?"

"Bad news travels fast," Larry commented. "But, of course, I forgot; you and Maddalena are pretty thick, aren't you? Personally, I should be very careful with that young woman. My guess is she hasn't much time for the male sex."

"She has for me," Carlo said and flashed his brilliant white teeth.

Larry and Rita were invited to dine with friends that evening. He had begun to feel off-colour again during the drive back to the Villa but decided to try and hide the fact from Rita so as not to spoil her evening. His headache and sickness increased as he was changing and when he went out to meet her on the terrace, she was at once aware that he was unwell. Instantly she was full of concern.

"I'll ring up and say we can't come. The Sirelli's won't mind, I'm sure."

Larry was insistent on Rita going without him. It would only make him feel worse, he said, if he knew he had ruined her evening too. "I'll go to bed with a book. I'm sure I'll be all right when I lie down."

In the end Rita let herself be persuaded. Before she left, however, she went out to the kitchen and prepared his glass of hot milk, bringing it out to him herself.

Larry sat on the terrace with the glass on the table beside him. He heard the engine of Rita's car start up in the garage at the other side of the house and then gradually die away into the distance.

The cat, Troilus, leapt from nowhere onto the terrace and sat at his feet, staring alternately at Larry's eyes and the glass of milk. Inside the house the telephone was ringing. He poured a little of the milk into the saucer and set it on the ground in front of the cat.

"A gentleman on the telephone would like to speak to you, sir," Maddalena's voice coming from the darkness behind made him start.

"Oh! Who is it?"

"He would not give any name, sir."

Larry crossed the terrace and lifted the receiver in the now gloomy sitting room.

"Mr Conway?" The voice was strong and vibrant but completely unknown to Larry.

"Yes."

"Just a friendly warning. Don't drink that glass of milk."

"Who the devil ..." Larry began, but a click told him that the line was already dead.

Scratching his chin, he went slowly back to the terrace. The glass stood on the table, still steaming slightly. On the ground, Troilus sat beside the half-finished saucer of milk. Larry stooped and placed it under the animal's nose. It backed away. He tried to force the cat's face towards the milk, urging it to drink. Suddenly, its claws came out, lashing at Larry's hand. With a wild cry, the cat vanished into the darkness.

# EPISODE THREE

Larry stood for several minutes staring into the night where the cat had disappeared. The throbbing sound of a cicada in a nearby tree seemed to fill the night; far below the lights of fishing boats winked on the water. He emptied the remains of the glass of milk over the edge of the terrace, then carried the saucer and tumbler right through the house and into the kitchen.

Maddalena looked up in surprise. It was rare for the master to invade her domain.

"That was a very nice glass of milk, Maddalena. Did you prepare it for me?"

"No, sir. The mistress insisted on doing it herself."

Larry took a book up to bed with him, but he did not read it. It lay open on his chest whilst he stared at the patterned wallpaper on the ceiling. He simply could not bring himself to believe that Rita was trying to poison him. It just did not make sense. From a financial point of view, he was the one who would benefit by her death, not she by his. Could there be any other motive?

Had he been living in a fool's paradise; believe he had won Rita's affection while all the time she was in love with someone else and only waiting for a chance to be rid of him? The thought hurt terribly; his mind veered away from it only to fix on another disturbing riddle.

What had become of Lewis Sanderstead? Except that he was American and that his money came from oil, Larry knew practically nothing about him. Rita never spoke of him but everyone in Portofino seemed to have liked him. Where and how had he died? The only definite fact was that it had not been here in Portofino.

He was still puzzling it out when he heard Rita's car on the drive. She had left the party early in order to hurry home.

Knowing that he could not look her in the eye, Larry hastily closed his book and turned his bedside light out. When Rita entered, he was pretending to be asleep. He sensed her bending over him, studying his face carefully. She made practically no sound as she prepared for the night and slid into bed.

He was very silent as they breakfasted on the terrace next morning. His fears of the previous evening seemed ludicrous against the brilliance of the morning – the intense blue of the sea, the velvety green of the pines and the dazzling whiteness of the villas.

Rita herself was so lovely and fresh, so genuinely concerned about him. "You're very silent, my darling. How are you feeling this morning?"

"Not too good, I'm afraid."

Her face clouded. She stretched her hand across the table and took his.

"Larry, I'm terribly worried about you. You did take your milk last night?"

"Yes," Larry lied. "I don't think it's doing me much good, though."

"I'll ring up Mario. He ought to see you again."

"Oh, it's not as bad as all that. I expect all I need is a bit of exercise. I'll stroll down to Portofino later this morning and get my hair cut."

Larry had already made up his mind that he would call on Ricola at his clinic. He wanted to have the opportunity of asking him some questions without fear of interruption.

He saw that the doctor was surprised when the receptionist showed him into the consulting room.

"I don't want Rita to know about this," he explained, "she'd only worry. But the fact is, I'd be a lot easier in my own mind if you'd give me a thorough overhaul – put the ruler over me from top to toe."

Ricola hesitated only a second. His fashionable practice had not been built up by scoffing at the anxieties of his patients.

"I would be delighted. Just slip your shirt off and lie down on that couch."

It was a purely formal procedure and perhaps both of them knew it. As he lay on the leather couch, Larry brought the conversation round to Rita's first husband. He thought he detected a trace of irony in Ricola's voice as he described how popular Lewis Sanderstead had been.

"One wonders if he wasn't just a little too good to be true." As to the cause of his death, Ricola was as ignorant as Larry.

"You hadn't treated him for any illness at all, then?"

"Well," Ricola admitted, "I did examine him once when he complained of pains in the stomach."

"And what was your diagnosis?"

"It's always hard to diagnose such pains – but at the time I put it down to food poisoning."

"Was this shortly before Lewis and Rita left Portofino for the last time?"

"Yes, it was. Indeed, it was in the hope that Lewis's health would improve that they undertook that trip to the United States."

After leaving the doctor, Larry strolled down through narrow winding streets drenched with sunlight towards the animated little harbour.

He was musing on what Ricola had told him, trying to make sense of the peculiar behaviour of the cat Troilus and the mysterious voice which had spoken to him on the telephone. Someone in Portofino seemed to know more about what went on in the Villa Serena than he did himself.

Some persistent quality in the footsteps at the back made him turn his head. The man walking some ten yards behind him was dressed in a light tropical suit and was wearing a Panama hat. He appeared to be unaware of his surroundings and as he walked along, he was reading a small paper-backed book. There was something familiar about him, yet Larry could not recall where he had seen him before.

As he turned in at the door of his hairdresser's, the stranger went past. Glancing up from his book, he found Larry's eyes fixed on his face. He gave a half smile and went on down the street.

Sitting under the white sheet, staring at his own reflection in the mirror, Larry tried to place the stranger but was forced to admit defeat. His mind was so obsessed by his besetting problem that this minor one soon went out of his head.

He had decided now what he would do. That evening he would preserve a sample of milk and have it analysed. And supposing it really did contain poison? Supposing analysis confirmed that Rita was trying to poison him – what then?

The barber was brushing stray hairs off his coat when a small urchin burst into the shop and handed Larry a note scribbled on a sheet torn from a notebook. He tipped the boy and unfolded the paper.

'*You are quite right. You have seen me before. Why don't we have a drink at the café on the quay? I should like to express my sympathy.*'

Larry stared at the sloped handwriting. He absently felt in his pocket for money and gave the barber an unintentionally generous tip. The man rushed to open the door and bow him out.

The quay was only a few steps away. He turned unhesitatingly towards it – his curiosity aroused by the wording of the note. Where had he seen this stranger before and why on earth should he wish to offer his sympathy?

The figure in the tropical suit was not in the café. Staring across the harbour, Larry spotted him outside a bar which provided cushions so that drinks could be taken sitting on the quay. The man with the Panama hat was squatting on the flagstones with his back to the bar wall.

As Larry approached, he looked up and smiled but did not attempt to rise.

Larry said: "Did you send me this note?"

The stranger nodded. "Yes. I did. Mr Conway, I should like to express my sympathy."

Larry frowned. "Your sympathy?"

"Yes, my dear fellow. About Troilus – he was such a charming cat."

"I don't understand you. What's happened to Troilus?"

The stranger smiled. "He's dead. I think he drank some milk that didn't agree with him."

# EPISODE FOUR

Larry was at the same time shaken and infuriated by the calm announcement. The implication behind the stranger's words was unmistakable and the voice was the same – this was the man who had telephoned him the previous evening.

"You seem to know a damn sight too much," he said angrily.

"It is my business to know what goes on at the Villa Serena, Mr Conway. For instance, I know that you have not been feeling too well lately."

"It was you who telephoned me last night, wasn't it?"

The stranger nodded.

"Then don't you think you owe me an explanation? Just who are you and what are you doing here?"

For answer, the man patted the cushion at his side and invited Larry to sit down. He hesitated, then he too squatted on the ground, his back to the wall. The stranger raised a finger and caught the waiter's eye.

"Bring this gentleman an orange juice," he said.

"*Si signore.*"

"Waiter!" Larry's angry voice halted the man before he had gone two paces. "Make it a dry martini."

The stranger laughed softly.

"Now," Larry turned towards him, "you seem to know my name. Don't you think it's time I knew yours?"

"My name is Quinter. Richard Quinter."

"And may I know why you are so interested in the Villa Serena?"

"Because I am interested in Mrs Sanderstead … forgive me! I should say Mrs Conway. You see, I knew her first husband so well that I always think of her by that name."

"If you knew Lewis Sanderstead so well, perhaps you can answer this question: how did he die?"

Quinter met Larry's eyes steadily over the rim of his cocktail glass.

"He was poisoned, Mr Conway."

Larry felt sick when he heard this news. Quinter's confident statement gave substance to the fear which had begun to haunt him. He stared at the man with hatred as he sat there on his gaily coloured cushion, blandly sipping a cocktail. There was something efficient and calculating about him that was out of place in this idyllic setting – the white yachts nodding on the blue-green waters, the gay music from a café loudspeaker, the warm friendly sunshine.

The waiter brought Larry's martini and he drank two-thirds of it at the first sip.

"What made you think that my glass of milk was poisoned?"

"I know that your wife is trying to poison you."

Larry set his glass down so violently that the stem almost shattered. His hand was trembling with anger. To formulate a suspicion in his own mind was one thing; to hear a stranger make this accusation against Rita was quite another matter.

"That's a damnable thing to say – and utterly untrue. Rita and I ..."

Quinter was shaking his head, completely unmoved by Larry's outburst.

"I have been watching her for some time. I knew that she would eventually find another victim."

"You've been watching her for some time? What are you – a detective?"

"I'm a friend of Lewis Sanderstead's," Quinter replied, avoiding the question, "and a friend of yours, Mr Conway."

Larry scrambled to his feet and stood looking down at him.

"Your suggestion is completely ridiculous. What possible reason could Rita have for trying to poison me?"

Quinter nodded, eyeing Larry with that same maddening expression of confident knowledge.

"That's the big question, Mr Conway. That's one even I can't figure out."

"When you do," Larry remarked with sarcasm, "let me know."

He turned on his heel and walked off the quay.

As he climbed up the winding path that made a short cut to the villa, he felt a stab of pain in his stomach and was forced to stop and rest. Through a gap in the trees, he could see the harbour and the quay. Quinter had vanished. Larry was becoming convinced that the man was a detective of some kind. It was unlikely, however, that he was a member of Scotland Yard or the F.B.I. Then by whom was he employed? Could it be some relation of Rita's late husband who was not satisfied with the manner of Sanderstead's death?

Larry was only just in time for lunch. Rita was waiting for him on the terrace. The cocktail trolley had been wheeled out as usual, but he noticed that the bottle of Italian gin had been removed. Rita made him sit down with a long glass of iced Carpano and soda. She lit a cigarette and placed it between his lips. Every action seemed prompted by affection for his well-being.

That afternoon she took him down to the beach in her car. As they bathed in the cool water and relaxed in the sun, Larry felt that he and Rita had never been closer.

All through dinner he had the same sense of harmony. They talked again of that first meeting in Naples and the magic moment in Sorrento when she had come back to find him in a café. Only later, when they were taking coffee on the terrace, did the storm clouds blow up again. Larry wanted some final confirmation of his newly found faith in Rita and perhaps unwisely he brought the conversation round to Lewis Sanderstead.

"Did he have any idea that the end was near, Rita? Or was it quite sudden?"

He saw Rita stiffen and stare fixedly into the darkness.

"Must you keep bringing his name up? You know I'd rather not talk about it. What's past is past."

There was an awkward little silence between them. She made a deliberate effort to break it with a light remark.

"I think Troilus must have found his lady friend at last. We haven't seen him today."

When bedtime came, Rita went out to the kitchen and came back with Larry's glass of hot milk. He told her that he wasn't sleepy yet and would follow her up to bed when the milk had had time to make him drowsy.

Left alone, Larry went to his desk in the sitting room and took out an old flask which he had washed out in readiness. The neck was small, but he managed to pour enough milk into it to serve his purpose. He screwed it up tight, wiped it clean, then poured the rest of the milk over the edge of the terrace wall.

Next morning, he felt fitter than he had done for a long time. Once again, he walked down to the village and called on Dr Ricola. He handed him the flask and asked him to test the contents. The doctor looked surprised but did as he was asked. When he returned from his little laboratory, his face was grave.

"I have had a positive result," he said. "This milk contains a small quantity of arsenic."

"Enough to kill someone?"

"Not in one dose. The proportion of poison is very small. But such doses taken over a period of time would eventually prove fatal."

Larry was silent, his thoughts in a turmoil. The doctor said quietly: "Where does this milk come from? I shall have to report this matter to the authorities at once. If there is some contamination of the supply ..."

"The supply's not contaminated. The poison was deliberately put in my milk."

"Good God! Then there's all the more reason –"

Larry took the doctor's arm. "Listen, Mario. I want you to say nothing about this for twenty-four hours. I promise I'll keep you informed, but I must have one day's grace."

With obvious reluctance, Ricola agreed. When Larry had gone, he had sat down heavily at his desk and unlocked a drawer. He took out a large, framed photograph of Rita Sanderstead and sat frowning at it for a long time.

Back at the Villa, Larry was met by Maddalena. The mistress was out, she informed him, but a letter had been delivered by hand for him an hour ago.

He took it into the sitting room and waited until he was alone before he opened it. The handwriting was Quinter's.

"I've discovered the answer to your question, Mr Conway, *I know why.* I suggest we lunch at Romano's – one o'clock.

RICHARD QUINTER"

# EPISODE FIVE

Larry crumpled the note up and thrust it into his pocket. He rang the bell to summon Maddalena. "I shall be out to lunch, Maddalena. If the mistress returns, tell her I had a sudden message from a friend."

Quinter had not yet arrived at Romano's, but he had reserved a table on the pavement outside under the arcades. Carlo showed Larry to his place and brought the usual martini. He sat impatiently smoking, wishing that Quinter would show up.

Presently, he saw the tall, lean figure strolling along between the palm trees. Quinter was reading the same paperbacked book and had the air of a man who has all the time in the world. He looked up and saw Larry and crossed the road towards him.

"I got your note," Larry said, and his disquiet was betrayed by his husky voice. "What's this news you have for me?"

"*Buon giorno, Carlo.*" Quinter greeted the waiter who had hurried over with the menu. It was clear that he was already well known at Romano's.

Before he answered Larry's question, he insisted on ordering lunch – scampi, a *saltinbocca alla Romano* and strawberries and cream. He selected a Ruffino chianti from the wine list and only when Carlo had gone posthaste to the kitchen, shouting the order as he went, did Quinter turn to Larry.

"Yes, Mr Conway, I know why your wife is trying to poison you."

Larry did not answer.

"For some time now," Quinter went on, "I have known that she was planning to get rid of you, but I could not discover why. In seventy out of every hundred murders committed, the motive is financial gain.

"But that could not apply in this case. Mrs Sanderstead would gain nothing by your death. Jealousy provides the motive for another ten per cent. But Rita knows as well as you do that you haven't looked at another woman since you married her."

"You seem to know a devil of a lot about me," Larry grunted.

Quinter smiled but did not deny the truth of this remark. "The motive in this instance is a simple one – no woman likes to be made a fool of."

Larry stared at him. With a sudden awful clarity, he saw himself from a completely new point of view.

"Yes," Quinter said, "you've guessed it. For some time now she has known all about you – what you were before she took you up, your elaborate plans to make her acquaintance, your bogus rescue in Naples. Outwardly, she appears to be as fond of you as ever, but secretly she is hating you and despising you for what you are – an imposter."

Quinter's words were like the lash of a whip.

"That is why she is trying to murder you."

His eyes left Larry's only when Carlo came to stand at his elbow.

"You are wanted on the telephone, Mr Quinter."

"Excuse me, Mr Conway."

Quinter laid his napkin down and pushed his chair back. When he was gone, Larry stared at the dish of prawns. He did not want to eat. Nor did he want to hear any more of what Quinter had to say. He left a tip for Carlo, got up from the table and walked quickly to his car.

He drove slowly back along the narrow, winding road to Portofino. How often had he made up his mind to tell Rita the whole truth and how often had he lacked the courage to do so.

Now it was too late. Useless now to tell her that he had never dreamed he was capable of feeling the affection she had inspired in him.

"I asked for this," he told himself fiercely. "I damned well asked for it."

Well, there was obviously only one thing for him to do. It was by his own volition that he had entered Rita's life and he could leave it in the same way. If he disappeared now, he would save them both; there was little doubt that Ricola would suspect the truth if he were to die of poisoning.

But if Larry were simply to disappear, he was sure that Ricola would remain silent. Larry would at least have known three years of perfect happiness.

By the time he reached the Villa, his plan was formed. Rita had returned home and was in the sitting room. They had hardly seen anything of each other all day and she appeared almost over-anxious to talk to him and find out how he really was. Rather clumsily, he excused himself and went to his dressing room. He packed a suitcase with the things he usually took on a journey and cautiously took it down the back stairs and out to the car.

Dinner was a tense meal. He knew that he was not capable of covering his real feelings for Rita. She had noticed his sombre mood and was trying to shake him out of it by her gayness and attentiveness.

When they had moved to the sitting room and Maddalena was serving the coffee, Rita suddenly rose and went to her desk. She came back with a small leather box.

"I have a little surprise for you."

"What's this?"

"Don't you remember? What day is it? It's exactly three years since the night I abandoned the *Queen of Orleans* to come back and join you."

Larry took the box and opened it. Inside, reposing on a bed of cotton wool, was a pair of gold cufflinks. Rita's eyes were shining; there was a trace of moisture in them.

"Rita darling – how sweet of you."

Suddenly, Larry wanted to blurt the whole thing out to her – his ridiculous fears, his own deceitfulness. Then he realised that Maddalena was standing at the door watching. This could be a carefully staged scene. If anything happened to Larry, Maddalena would be a convenient witness to indicate that the master and mistress were on the best of terms.

Robbed of words, he sat there while Rita bent to kiss him. She went out to the kitchen and returned with his glass of milk. "I'm so glad you're feeling better, darling. I'm going to bed now, but I'll be waiting upstairs."

Larry sat and stared at the glass of milk. In his mind, he went again over his conversation with Quinter and the events of the last few days.

"My God!" he thought. "You never know what is going on in a woman's mind."

Suddenly, he rose and looked at his watch. He walked quietly into the Villa and went out through the back door that led to the garages. He stood for a moment in the courtyard, looking back at the house. The moon was just rising, sending slanting beams of misty light through the pines. Behind the Venetian blinds, the light in Rita's room shone steadily and brightly.

With an effort he turned towards the garage. The door was open. A shaft of moonlight shone over his shoulder and illuminated the car.

Sprawled across the bonnet was the body of Dr Ricola, the handle of a stiletto sticking out from under his heart.

# EPISODE SIX

Dr Ricola's face was turned towards Larry, his teeth bared. His assailant had obviously forced him back against the car and then used the stiletto.

The shock of seeing that rigid face in the moonlight turned Larry momentarily to stone. A thousand thoughts raced through his mind and from them one emerged with crystal clarity; Rita has been with him the whole evening.

He shook his head like a swimmer after a dive and pulled himself together. He edged past Ricola and took a torch from the garage drawer. Then he backed out of the garage and slid the door shut. He stood for a moment in the darkness, wondering how far away the murderer was. There were the marks of a struggle on the path that led up through the trees.

Larry remembered that Ricola often left his car on the road below the Villa and took this short cut on foot. He slithered as fast as he could down to the road. Ricola's sky-blue Lancia was there, deserted and glinting in the moonlight.

Larry climbed back towards the Villa Serena, knowing that Ricola had been attacked on this same path shortly before he reached the courtyard. One very strong motive for this killing had already suggested itself to him. Ricola was the only person whom he had told about the poisoned milk. Even if it was impossible for Rita to have killed him, she could have got someone else to commit the murder for her.

He had wasted enough time already. It was urgent for him to notify the police at once if he was to avoid suspicion falling on himself. He entered the Villa, snapped on the sitting room lights and crossed to the telephone. He was about to call the police when a thought struck him. Quinter must be well versed in criminal matters and could advise him how to proceed. There was an outside chance that he might be at Romano's. He was fumbling about in the telephone book when Maddalena came in to investigate the sudden switching on of the lights.

"Maddalena, you must know the telephone number of Romano's – where your friend, Carlo, works."

"Santa Margherita 27, sir."

"Thanks," Larry had already picked up the receiver. "Ask the mistress to come down here at once, will you?"

An unknown voice answered from Romano's and it was some time before Carlo spoke. He seemed surprised at Larry ringing him up. Quinter, he said, had indeed been dining at Romano's but had just left. Carlo didn't know where Larry could find him. Larry thanked him. Just as he was about to replace the receiver, he heard a click in the earpiece.

Someone had been listening to the conversation on an extension line and had just replaced their instrument.

Larry had time to light a cigarette before Rita hurried in. She was wearing a silk dressing gown and in her hand she still carried the photograph album she had been looking at in bed.

"What on earth has happened, Larry? Have you had another of those attacks?"

"No," said Larry, "something much more serious than that."

Omitting only his reason for going out to the garage, he told her bluntly how he had found Ricola. She went deathly pale, felt for a chair and sank down.

"Now," Larry went on without taking his eyes from her face, "I'm going to telephone the police."

"Poor Mario. What a terrible thing!"

"You realise that they're going to start asking all sorts of questions? We shall both have to make statements under oath."

Larry paused, his hand on the instrument. He expected Rita to make some protest, to play for time. Instead, she stared back at him with a puzzled expression.

"Why do you keep looking at me like that?"

Suddenly, she put her hand to her throat. She rose from her chair as a look of disbelief and horror came over her face. The photograph album slipped unheeded to the floor.

"Larry, you don't ... you can't mean ... it wasn't you who killed Mario?"

Completely staggered by the suggestion, Larry stared back at her.

"Good God, no! Why on earth should I?"

"Oh, thank heaven for that! Why do you hesitate to ring the police then?"

"Because when they come, I shall have to tell them the truth – the whole truth. For instance, I shall have to tell them that I took a sample of my milk to Ricola this morning and that his analysis showed that it contained arsenic."

"Arsenic? You mean – poison?"

"Yes."

Her shock and bewilderment seemed completely unfeigned. Indeed, he had to steady her, or she would have fallen.

"But I brought it to you myself. How could it have been poisoned?"

"I don't know, but I think it's time the police were notified."

She nodded, her eyes still wide with shock. "Yes, you must call the police."

Larry stood, waiting for the exchange to answer. He was standing behind Rita and could see only the top of her head and the rise and fall of her bosom. Was it genuine concern and grief that moved her so deeply or was she afraid because now the police were about to be involved?

At last, the operator answered.

"Get me the police, please. It's urgent."

Larry's eyes moved to the floor. The photograph album lay open at his feet where it had fallen. This anniversary had clearly prompted Rita to go back over the old times. There were pictures of Naples, Pompeii and Sorrento – some of Larry, some of Rita, a few of them both together. There was even one showing them sitting at their favourite café where they had returned simply so that they could be photographed there. Memories came flooding back to Larry with painful vividness. Everything has been so beautiful and simple then as they were carried away on the tide of their happiness. What a contrast to this present misery. In a few minutes now the whole fragile myth would be destroyed.

His eyes moved to the opposite page of the album. It was covered by photographs which had been taken during Rita's cruise on the *Queen of Orleans*. One of them showed Rita standing on the promenade deck with a youngish woman and two men. One of the men was holding Rita's arm and looking quite pleased with himself.

Larry stiffened. His attention was attracted by the Panama hat which the man held in his free hand. He bent down to pick the album up. The face swam towards him, its features unmissable in the clear sunlight of that day just over three years ago.

"Quinter!"

# EPISODE SEVEN

The sound of an official voice in his ear jerked Larry back to reality. "This is Mr Conway calling from the Villa Serena. Can you come at once, please? Dr Ricola has been killed – murdered."

There was a moment's silence, then the voice said: "We will come at once, Signor Conway. Meantime, you will please see that nothing is touched and that no one leaves your house."

He replaced the receiver and picked the photograph album off the floor.

"Are they coming at once?" Larry did not even hear Rita's question. He was staring at Quinter's photograph. What had the man been doing on the *Queen of Orleans*? He certainly looked very sure of himself and remarkably friendly towards Rita.

"Larry!" He looked up and found that Rita was questioning him. "What were you doing down at the garage at this time of night?"

"Before I answer that I want you to tell me something. Who is this man?"

"But darling! What a question to ask me at a time like this!"

"Who is he?"

Rita took the album and glanced casually at the photograph.

"He's a man called Michael Redland."

"He was on that cruise with you?"

"Yes."

"I want you to tell me all you know about him – it may be very important."

"But why? Do you think he may have had something to do with the murder?"

67

"I can't tell till I know more about him. Were you very friendly with him?"

"It was rather a case of him being friendly with me. It wasn't an isolated case, you know. More than one man has wooed me for my wealth."

Larry dropped his eyes, but Rita was looking at him without animosity.

"I was warned by someone who knew him that he was only after me for my money. It was no disappointment to me. I'd met you by that time and I was in love."

"With another imposter," said Larry quietly.

"Yes, darling, I know that now. Redland took good care to write and inform me that you were a card-sharper and a gambler and were after my money. He was furious at you for succeeding where he had failed."

"Did you believe him?"

"I wasn't interested. I was in love with you."

"But did you believe him?" Larry persisted.

"I had some inquiries made and got to know a great deal more about you than you realised. That didn't worry me. You see, I believed that you were in love with me in spite of yourself. Having lived for four years with a man who was quite indifferent to me I rather enjoyed the experience."

She closed the photograph album and looked up at him with a smile. "I've never regretted our marriage for one moment."

The tramp of booted feet in the hall saved Larry from having to speak. A police Inspector with a squad of minions seemed to suddenly fill the entire landscape. Briefly Larry gave him particulars of where the body was and how he had found it.

"First I shall want to see the body," the Inspector said. "Then I shall want to question everyone in your household. No one must leave the building."

He took himself away towards the garage.

For a few minutes Larry and Rita were left alone again. She spoke in a low voice with swift urgency.

"Larry, you told the Inspector that you went down to the garage because you were going away for a few days. That wasn't true, was it?"

"Yes," Larry said, "it was true. Only I wasn't going for a few days. I was leaving for good."

"But why? What have I done?"

"I'm afraid I have a lot to confess to you."

He had decided to tell her the whole story. As he described how the suspicion had grown in his mind that she had been trying to kill him, she watched his face with frank disbelief.

"And you believed all this?"

"I didn't want to, but as one thing followed another – then the analysis of the milk."

"You actually believe that I was capable of poisoning you?"

To Larry's relief the humiliating scene was interrupted by the return of the Inspector. He demanded to see Larry's hands and asked him to roll his shirt sleeves up to his elbow.

"What's this in aid of?"

The Inspector seemed satisfied and answered Larry's questions.

"We have reconstructed the crime. A struggle took place on the path. Dr Ricola managed to elude his attacker and take refuge in the garage. There he was trapped and killed. You heard no shouts, no cry for help?"

"No. We had the radio on during dinner."

"I see. Unintentionally, perhaps, the doctor managed to wound his attacker. We found his bag in the bushes. The sharp edge of the clasp bore bloodstains. The murderer obviously must have ripped his hand or arm on it."

Larry hardly listened. He was watching Rita who had turned her face away and would not look in his direction. An unsurmountable barrier seemed to separate them now. He could see that she was deeply wounded.

The Inspector's monologue was interrupted by the sound of excited voices outside the window. All three turned as the door was opened and two *carabinieri* brought in a scared looking Maddalena. From the voluble explanation, Larry gathered that she had been caught trying to slip away.

Her legs were scratched and there were patches of dirt on her cheeks. She was still in her working clothes, except that her apron had been removed. Her lips pouted and her eyes were sullen as she stood there. Watching her closely, Larry came to the conclusion that she was very frightened.

"You heard my orders that no one was to leave the Villa?" the Inspector demanded.

Maddalena nodded.

"Then why did you disobey?"

"I went to post a letter."

"To post a letter? And can you show me this letter?"

Maddalena was silent. She had no letter to show. The Inspector advanced to the attack.

"You are lying! This is a serious matter. A man has been murdered. You are found attempting to escape in the darkness. It will be bad for you unless you tell the truth."

Larry stepped forward. "Can I have a word with her, Inspector?"

The Inspector nodded grudgingly. Larry turned to Maddalena and spoke to her urgently.

"There is no need for you to be frightened, Maddalena. Just take your time and answer the Inspector's questions when you are ready. You are excited and over-wrought."

The Italian seemed to relax a little, but she was still suspicious of Larry. He went on softly: "I want you to do something for me, Maddalena. Will you do it?"

"What is it, *signore*?" The girl was already drying her eyes.

Larry turned to the low table, where the glass with his milk had been placed an hour ago and where it had stood forgotten ever since. It was cold now and a wrinkly film covered the surface.

Larry handed Maddalena the glass. "I want you to drink this milk."

The girl stared at Larry then instinctively shrank back, holding up a hand between herself and the glass.

# EPISODE EIGHT

Suddenly realising she had betrayed herself, Maddalena clapped a hand to her mouth; her eyes moved round the circle of faces now watching in stunned silence.

Larry said softly: "So you were the one who was trying to poison me!"

"No, *signore, Por l'amor di Dio*, you must believe me." She had fallen on her knees and joined her hands in supplication before Larry. "I did not mean to kill you. They forced me to do it."

"You wouldn't have needed much forcing," said Larry. "You've obviously hated me from the very first moment I came here. But who do you mean when you say they? Quinter obviously, but who else?"

Maddalena's mouth clamped shut, but the Inspector shook her roughly by the shoulder.

"Speak, woman! Would you rather we took you to the police station for questioning?"

"It was Carlo," she whispered, then added illogically, "but it was not his fault. Signor Quinter bribed him."

Gradually, in bits and pieces, the whole story came out whilst Rita and Larry listened with growing amazement. The initial plan had been Quinter's. He had elicited the help of Carlo for two reasons; firstly, because he regularly served Larry with drinks and secondly because he had a hold over Maddalena, who already worked at the Villa Serena. Quinter had explained from the start that no real harm could come to Larry. The object was to provoke only the symptoms of slow poisoning. Carlo had begun the good work at Romano's by tampering with Larry's drinks and Maddalena had continued it by adding small quantities of arsenic to the bottle of milk which she placed in the refrigerator ready for Rita to prepare for Larry.

"And you still maintain you had no intention of killing me? What was the object of this elaborate game, then?"

Maddalena had realised now that there could be no drawing back. She cast Rita a terrified glance then dropped her eyes.

"Signor Quinter believed he could convince you that your wife was trying to poison you. Then he would have persuaded you that you could save yourself by killing her. You would have felt justified in doing this and you would have inherited all the money."

Rita gasped and sank back into a chair.

"Thoughtful of Mr Quinter," said Larry. "I'm sure he had dreamed up a nice tidy way for me to do it. And exactly what did he expect to gain from all this?"

"You would have been a rich man," Maddalena said simply. "He would have bled you of your money like a vampire."

It was Larry's turn to be shocked. It took him a moment to comprehend the full devilry of Quinter's plan. The squid who waits patiently in his rock hole till a prey comes within reach of its armoured tentacles had nothing to teach this man.

"But what about Troilus?" Larry demanded suddenly. "If the doses were so harmless, why did he die?"

"I killed him," Maddalena sobbed. "Signor Quinter made me do it. It was to make you believe ..."

"And who killed Dr Ricola?"

"I do not know. Not till I heard you telephone did I learn that he was dead. I was so frightened. I wanted to warn Carlo ..."

Larry turned to the Inspector. "It was Quinter. I'm convinced of it! He knew I would suspect Rita, that I'd jump to the conclusion she'd done it because Ricola knew about the poison in the milk. He could have telephoned the doctor, asked him to come to the Villa, then laid in wait for him on the path."

The Inspector asked: "You can give me a description of this man Quinter?"

"I can do more than that. I can show you his photograph."

The Inspector wasted little time after that. With one of his men dragging Maddalena along, he took his party out to the waiting cars. For a few minutes, the wood round the Villa echoed to the sound of racing engines. Then there was silence. Rita and Larry faced each other across the sitting room.

"Larry. How could you have allowed yourself to believe such a thing? After the wonderful years we had together?"

"I don't know. It seems madness now. But the diabolic part of Quinter's plan was that it worked on my guilty conscience. My mind was so full of the fact that I had played you false, and fully deserved all I got, that I couldn't really think straight. You know, men do find it hard to know what's going on in a woman's mind."

They were standing far apart and there was a coldness in her voice and manner that he had never encountered before. Larry thought: "Whatever happens to Quinter now, he's succeeded in one thing. He's robbed me of Rita."

Aloud he said: "You know, the evidence did point towards you. It was you who prepared the milk for me every evening and I was able to prove that it was poisoned."

"I brought it to you, yes," Rita admitted. "But Maddalena always had it in the saucepan ready."

"Oh," Larry was momentarily at a loss, but he went on putting his case desperately. "There was something else that made me wonder. Lewis – your first husband – had suffered the same pains and died mysteriously. You always seemed so secretive about him."

"*De mortuis nil nisi bonum*. Have you ever heard that?" Rita's voice was weary. "Now I suppose everything must be told!"

She faced him and spoke in mechanical, matter of fact tones.

"Lewis Sanderstead was a drunkard. He bullied me cruelly and was constantly unfaithful. On the surface he was charming, but when we were alone, he could become a devil. Mario knew nothing of this. Lewis sent for a doctor from Genoa to deal with his spells of delirium tremens."

"Good God!"

"Shortly after we arrived in the States that last time, he went on a drinking orgy and got a silly girl of eighteen to go out with him in his car. He was incapable of controlling it and they were both killed in a ghastly smash-up. The girl's family and I were able to hush the whole thing up and keep it out of the press.

"It wouldn't have done anyone any good to make the horrid business public, but since you insist on the facts there you have them. You can guess why I felt the need of a world cruise."

There was nothing Larry could say. He fumbled for a cigarette and listened to the sharp crack of Rita's shoes as she walked past him across the marble floor.

She stopped just before she reached the door. "I hope you are now satisfied that I'm not a murderess?"

The words struck like a whip. Larry reflected bitterly that this was the first time in three years that Rita and he had quarrelled. Abruptly, his mood of self-pity vanished. A black and sullen anger rose in him against the man who had done this to his life. It had taken an experience like this to make him realise what a difference Rita had made to his whole existence. Not only had she given him happiness but self-respect and a proper place in society. If she left him now he could not imagine how he would go on living. Yet he had to admit to himself that she had no reason to stick to him any longer.

His anger had to express itself in action of some sort. He must find Quinter and with his bare hands make him pay for what he had done.

He strode out through the hall, down to the courtyard and across to the car which still waited with a packed suitcase in the back. He drove down to Santa Margherita with reckless speed. He intended to force Carlo to tell him where to find Quinter. The statement that he had dined at Romano's had obviously been an alibi for Ricola's murder.

Santa Margherita was a mass of gay colour. The cafés were crowded and hundreds of people were out walking in the warm evening. Larry forced his way through them with a finger permanently on the horn button.

There was a crowd round Romano's. He pulled up and stood on the seat of the car to look over their heads. He was in time to see a struggling Carlo being carried out by four *carabinieri* and rammed into the back of a Black Maria. Of Quinter there was no sign.

# EPISODE NINE

Once the police van had been driven away, the crowd melted quickly. Romano's remained closed-up and dark, though the chairs and tables still stood on the pavement outside. There was no chance of tracing Quinter there.

Larry parked his car and went into one of the noisier and more popular cafés, where he knew there was a telephone booth. He *carabinieri* post at Portofino; he guessed the Inspector would set up his headquarters there.

"We have had every hotel and boarding house checked, and searched every café in Portofino and Santa Margherita," the officer told him. "There's no sign of Quinter!"

"Doesn't Carlo know where he is?"

"My men got nothing out of him at Romano's. Either he does not know or is too frightened to talk. They're bringing him in now and we'll get to work on him again."

It was nearly midnight as Larry made his way back to the car, but the cafés were still buzzing with life. The sudden fury that had driven him from the Villa had died.

In its place had grown a colder, more reasoning anger. The sense that he had lost Rita was a constant goad to his determination to find Quinter.

He tried to put himself in the other man's shoes. Quinter, he believed, must have foreseen that Larry might simply decide to go away and leave Rita for good. That would have suited his book perfectly well. He could reappear in the role of guide, counsellor and friend to Rita and continue the good work he had begun on the *Queen of Orleans*.

It had probably not been part of his original plan to murder Ricola, but even that would not have endangered him seriously if Maddalena had not broken down. The arrival of the police to arrest Carlo would have been his first warning that all his plans had gone seriously amiss.

For all these reasons he felt sure that Quinter was still near at hand.

"If I were trying to sneak out of here," Larry thought, "which way would I go? Sea? Too complicated unless I'd arranged it beforehand. Road? Too dangerous – the police almost certainly have checks out."

Then he remembered the steep road which winds up the side of the natural bowl that encloses Santa Margherita harbour. It joined the main highway from La Spezia to Genoa about a thousand feet above sea level.

"It's the only way out. That's the way I'd go if I were on the run."

He started his car and headed for the hill road. Tyres squealed as he spun the low-built Ferrari round hairpin after hairpin. He stopped at the top of a series of vicious bends and pulled the car to the side of the road. The almost sheer hillside had been cut into a series of terraces where the peasants grew their vines. Each one provided a brief step of level soil, shored up by precipitous walls. The effect was of a giant staircase.

Looking down over the terraces, Larry could see the road snaking below. The night was clear. Lights twinkled away down in the bay. Now and again the sound of a car horn floated up to him and once the far-off shriek of a train whistle. Several times he saw cars come nosing up the hill, their lights swinging now to landward, now to seaward. Each time he started his own car up and peered at the driver as the vehicle laboured past.

After half an hour, he began to feel certain that he had missed Quinter. Either he had already passed this way or had found some other hole in the net. Larry knew that the sensible thing for him to do was to go back to the Villa and leave the police to do their own work. His proper place was with Rita.

The real reason why he was sitting here, he admitted to himself, was because he dared not return to the Villa Serena in case he should find that she had gone.

He was abruptly aware that a car was on the road below. It was coming up very fast, engine racing and tyres screaming. As it passed the section of road just below him, he saw that it was a sky-blue Lancia convertible – Ricola's car! So this was where Quinter had been all this time, lying low within a few feet of the scene of the crime.

Larry leapt for his car. As the headlights of the Lancia blazed up the road from the bend behind, he pulled out. He had no doubts that Quinter would recognise Rita's scarlet Ferrari. He would then have to choose whether to stop or to pass.

Quinter slowed, the glare of his lights silhouetting the red car. Round several bends, he was almost bumping Larry's tail. It was clear that he meant to pass. On a short straight section, he drew alongside the Ferrari and began to close over on it, forcing it towards the outside of the road and the sheer drop. Larry bore down on his own steering wheel, the two cars locked, spun and crashed against the rock face on the inside of the road.

Quinter half-leapt and was half-thrown from his seat. When he picked himself up, he found Larry in the road waiting for him. There, in the reflected glare of the headlights, the two men faced each other.

Quinter was frightened and desperate, all his calm assurance gone. The big patch of sticking plaster on his right hand shone white and accentuated his movement as he reached for the automatic in his pocket.

Larry hit him with a flying tackle and the gun clattered on the road. The two men rolled on the black tarmac, silent except for their panting breath. Both of them knew that the choice was simple – kill or be killed.

Absorbed in their death struggle, they were unaware of the convoy of cars chasing up the hill below. Quinter, his strength failing and his breath stopped by an iron grip on his throat, managed to dig a knee into Larry's stomach and twist free. He scrambled to his feet and began to run down the road.

He was faced by a pair of glaring headlights as the first police car rounded the bend and jerked to a halt, barring his way. He spun round and saw Larry closing in on him from behind.

He turned and ran towards the low wall that separated the road from the black emptiness beyond. Perhaps if he had jumped straight down, he would have escaped with a couple of broken legs. Instead, swerving to avoid Larry, he caught his foot as he leapt. His body twisted as it fell.

Larry heard the crack of bone against stone. Staring down, he saw the motionless body, the head wrenched to a crazy angle.

A dozen police slithered down towards the dead man. Larry turned away. The craving for revenge was gone and now only emptiness remained in his heart.

He drove home slowly and left his car at the place where Ricola had so often parked his. He walked up through the woods, hoping to see a light in the house ahead. The Villa Serena was in complete darkness, though the door was open.

He passed through the hall and climbed the stairs to the bedroom. It was empty, impersonally tidy. The bedclothes had not even been turned down. The only trace of Rita was a faint tang of perfume.

"Oh well," he murmured. "I didn't expect anything else."

Before leaving the Villa for ever he wanted to take one last look from the terrace, where he and Rita had spent some of their happiest hours. He did not turn the sitting room lights on as he went out through the French window. A cool breeze was blowing up from the sea, stirring the pines. He stared ahead of him, reliving his past life like a drowning man. The craving for a cigarette came suddenly. He felt in his pocket, but the packet had fallen out in his struggle with Quinter.

Close behind him he heard a light step. He stood, frozen into immobility. A slim hand was placed over his eyes and a half-smoked cigarette was put between his lips.

A voice which he knew whispered: "Welcome home, darling."

Larry knew then that Fate had given him a second chance.

82

# RIGHT INTO THE HEART

(Translated from the German by Mike Linane)
A magazine serial
in nine episodes

## EPISODE ONE

Someone fired three shots.

The noise was short. Ugly. Dry. A ricochet hissed past Michael's head and slapped into the plaster of the scenery wall.

They hadn't heard the car coming. Now its engine howled as it sped away.

"My God, what was that?" the press officer gasped. When the sound popped, he had ducked down and covered his face with his hands.

"It sounded like gun shots," said Michael. "What do you think? Or a car back-firing or something?" He broke away from the other man and jumped towards Karin Lund. Her eyes were wide open, her mouth looked as if she was about scream. She trembled.

Michael grabbed her by the shoulders.

"Are you all right? Were you hurt?"

She shook her head.

"It's ok, take it easy," he said, upset for Karin as she let out a loud scream. "It's all right."

She nodded silently.

"You don't know each other yet," murmured the press officer. "This is Michael Collins, film reporter at the *Evening Comet*."

"All right," Michael interrupted him. "We don't have to go into all that now. Go to the nearest phone and ring for the police. I'll stay here."

"No," Karin said. "Please don't..."

Michael saw that she quickly glanced at the press officer who hesitated, not sure what to do.

"What – why not?" asked Michael.

"Not the police," she said slowly. "Nothing happened..."

Michael looked at her with his journalist's eyes. She was medium-height, slim and blonde, and as far as he could see, everything she had was sitting in the right place. He had liked her from the very first moment he saw her. But he usually felt that way with many movie stars, and it changed when he got to know them better.

Her grey-green eyes were unfathomable.

He took his eyes off her and turned his head to the press officer.

"What?" he said. "Are you telling me that was just a trick of yours? A novel way to introduce a foreign movie star to England? Damned original..."

His brows furrowed.

The other man raised his arms and nervously moved his glasses.

"What on earth makes you think that?" he said. "The bullets were real. You can see that as well as me."

"Hm," said Michael thoughtfully. "You're right." He turned to Karin Lund again. "And why don't you want the police sent for..."

"I already told you – nothing happened."

"What?" he asked. "Nothing happened? You're barely in London for a few days, and you're being shot at. And you say nothing happened? What do you call something like that in Sweden?"

He saw that her face darkened at what he said. Nevertheless, he said to the press officer: "Do it now – call the police! Otherwise, you can read about it tomorrow in the *Comet* that you didn't lift a finger in an attempted murder on your company's premises. You know what that is, man? Allowance. Aiding and abetting a crime."

The press officer gave him an uncertain look, turned and walked away.

"You are rude," said Karin Lund. She had overcome her shock. Her voice sounded cool.

"I don't understand you," Michael said. "Maybe I shouldn't even try to. Who knows what's behind all this?" He realised that his harshness upset her and said calmly, "Understand me, Miss Lund, that maniac could have hit you, and then..."

She read the apprehension in his eyes, and a tiny smile scurried across the corners of her mouth.

"I don't want any fuss," she said. "I have my reasons for doing so, believe me."

Michael grabbed her by the arm. "Be reasonable, Miss Lund. I'm not asking out of curiosity. I want to help you. Do these reasons have anything to do with the assassination attempt on you?"

She dodged his gaze. "I don't even know who shot at me..."

She turned around.

Someone was screaming.

A cry of horror...

Fifteen metres away from them, in front of the iron door to the studio floor, stood the press officer. He waved his arms. His face was full of shock and horror.

A moment later Michael joined him. Karin Lund ran after him.

"What is it?" asked Michael. "What's happened?"

The press officer pointed to the open door. Drops of sweat were running down his forehead.

"In there..." he choked. "In there – Mason!"

Michael rushed past him. Into the corridor that led to the studio.

Then he saw him.

It was lying on the bare cement floor. The body of a man in a blue tailor-made suit. A hand was on his chest. Where his heart was.

His head was on its side. On the black hair were chalky traces. He must have grazed the wall while falling before hitting the floor. And his eyes were open, and in them was the horror...

Michael took a moment to take a deep breath and then knelt down. He touched the hand lying on the man's chest, lifted it and dropped it...

He didn't need to check for a pulse. He'd already known at first glance.

Gary Mason, England's most famous movie star, was dead.

Michael looked over his shoulder. The press officer's face twitched.

"What are you waiting for?" Michael shouted at him. "Call the police! Tell the producer that no one is to come in here. Go on, what are you waiting for?"

The other man ran away, along the corridor, and disappeared through a door into the studio hall.

Michael got up and brushed the dust off his trousers.

Karin Lund leant against the wall.

Her face was white. She bit her lips.

"Listen, Miss Lund," Michael said in an unusually stern voice for him. "In a few minutes, the people from Scotland Yard will be here. They will ask you a lot of questions. And they are not as easy to fob off as I am. What do you have to do with this? The shots were fired at you. Why?"

Karin's face hardened. "How do you know that? He's the one who is dead. Not me..."

Michael gave her a sharp look. "Don't talk nonsense," he said. "You know exactly what I'm talking about. Have you forgotten what you said just now?"

Instead of answering, she took a pack of cigarettes from her leather jacket. She held the packet in her hand, cast a shy glance at the corpse in front of her and turned away. She hesitated.

Michael saw that her hand was shaking, took the packet, pulled out a cigarette and put it between her lips.

"Just smoke," he said tonelessly. "If it's going to help to calm you down..."

He gave Karin a light and looked into her eyes over the flame.

"If I were you, I would talk," he said. He made an effort not to make his words sound harsh.

Karin took a deep puff from the cigarette. "Thank you," she said evasively.

"All right," said Michael. "So you don't want to talk. You want to pretend that you have nothing to do with this whole thing. Perhaps your silence is meant to mean that I have no right to interfere in your affairs. And maybe that's right. But the man lying there is not just anyone. You know that as well as I do. The police will have every reason to investigate what happened here just now. And sooner or later they will uncover what is really going on here."

He saw the despair that was in Karin's eyes: and suddenly he felt sorry for her.

He took her by the arm. "Come on," he said. "Let's go outside. The fresh air will do you good."

She looked at him gratefully and let him lead her out. She didn't look back at the corpse.

Outside, Karin took a deep breath and leaned against Michael. He put his arm around her and patted her gently, soothingly on the shoulder. It was like a silent promise not to betray her.

Michael felt as if only a few minutes had passed until two large dark cars appeared on the road between the studio backdrops. The cars stopped and several men got out. One of the two who had got out of the first car approached. He raised an eyebrow. "Hello," he said in a deep voice. "What are you doing here?"

Michael shook the outstretched hand. He nodded his head towards the iron door. "In there..." he said, without answering the question.

The other turned to Karin. "My name is Parker," he said. "I'm a Detective Inspector at Scotland Yard." He looked at her closely and turned to the door.

"Wait here," he said, before beckoning the other men to follow him.

They disappeared into the entrance of the studio.

Michael looked at Karin Lund. She smoked silently, in deep breaths and stared expressionlessly at the wall of the studio opposite.

A few minutes later, Parker reappeared in the doorway. "What happened?" he asked. Michael told him. "We were standing over there," he began.

Inspector Parker listened. Every now and then his eyes slid to Karin Lund.

"And no one remembers the licence plate of the car or recognised the man?"

"No. And the number plate was smeared," Michael said. "Probably intentionally."

Parker nodded. "Can you at least tell me what make of car..."

"Probably an old Austin, but I'm not quite sure."

Parker's attention was everywhere. Behind them, two men with a stretcher carried the body out to an ambulance, which had arrived.

Parker turned to Karin Lund. "You were Gary Mason's co-star in the film you were shooting? Had you noticed anything unusual lately? I mean, was he worried about anything? Was he in any kind of trouble? Is there anything you can tell me?"

"I don't know anything," she replied.

"That was a little too fast," thought Michael. He remained silent and watched Karin and the Inspector attentively. It did not escape him that Parker squinted his eyes for a moment.

"So if I've got the situation correct, you were standing there when the shots were fired," Parker said. "The car drove by here." He pointed his hand in the direction. "Mason must have been standing in the doorway here at that moment. So practically behind you."

Karin Lund nodded.

"We didn't even know he was there," she said tonelessly.

"Understand me correctly, Miss Lund," he said. "I'm just trying to reconstruct what happened. And I have to think of every possibility. Could it be that the shots perhaps were aimed at you?"

Karin Lund looked at him in amazement. "What makes you think that, Inspector?" she asked calmly.

Michael hadn't seen any of her films yet. But he decided in a moment that she was a good actress.

"I don't want to think that's the case," Parker said. "But as I told you, I have to make sure about and consider all the possibilities."

Karin shook her head vigorously.

"That's fine," Parker said. "That'll be all for now. If you want, you can go back to the studio or to your dressing room. I doubt filming will continue today."

Thoughtfully, he looked after Karin Lund as she walked away.

Michael followed his gaze. He winced when Parker suddenly asked, "Do you think she was telling the truth?"

"Why are you asking me that?" Michael lowered his gaze.

"I don't know. But something's wrong here. I've just got a feeling...," Parker said.

"Oh," Michael said. "You and your hunches..."

Parker fixed his gaze on Michael. "I've been around a long time. And slowly you develop a sixth sense when you've been in this profession long enough."

"The victim's name is Gary Mason," Michael said.

Parker muttered something that Michael didn't understand.

"And yet," he continued. "After talking to that girl, I can't get rid of the feeling..."

He fell silent.


Michael knew that Parker had already solved many cases by not believing in the simplest solution in the first place. He had always considered even the most unlikely possibilities. Perhaps he really had developed something like a sixth sense, without claiming to be a super detective as they appear in crime novels.

"I really want to know if she is telling the truth," Parker said again. He looked at Michael questioningly.

Michael thought about it in a flash.

At Oxford University, he and Tom Parker had been good friends. At the same time, they had been interested in criminology. Later, Parker had turned his hobby into a profession and ended up at Scotland Yard. Michael had actually wanted to become a crime reporter. But Ben Dickens had held that job at *The Comet* for twenty-five years. And he was young enough to keep it for another twenty years.

"You know," he said hesitantly. "When you're dealing with people from the film industry – what does truth mean? It's an illusory world. Not even the stories the publicity people put out to the press are real..."

"But you've been writing about films for years," Parker said. "I always thought you enjoyed it. You're successful..."

"That's right," said Michael, "but I don't particularly love the job."

"So why are you still doing it then?"

Michael thought about this for a moment. "Well, I suppose there's something in every profession that you don't like. But I get along well with my boss. I have some good friends among my colleagues. And I'm also paid decently." He shrugged his shoulders. "What more can I ask for?"

"Nothing really," Parker said. He looked at Michael with some scrutiny. "But you haven't answered my question yet. Do you have the impression that this Miss Lund is telling me the truth?"

"What do you want me to say? I'm just trying to make it clear to you how difficult it is to find out from these film people what is appearance and what is reality."

"But this Miss Lund seems to me to be quite real," Parker hummed. "And if I'm not mistaken, then you have taken note of it very well."

Michael's face darkened. "And what precisely do you mean by that?"

Parker pinned a keen eye on him. "Nothing – of course..." he said. "OK, I suppose I'd better go and talk to the press officer."

He left Michael standing without shaking his hand to say goodbye and trudged towards the entrance of the studio.

91

Michael watched him walk away until he was inside the studio door.

The large room with many desks and typewriters was busy with activity. Michael hung his hat on a hook and went to the editor's desk. Arthur Ford sucked peppermints and looked as desperate as ever at this time of day.

"I've got three-columns for tomorrow, maybe even the lead for page one," Michael called out to him.

"What's happened? The film studio burned down?" Ford cynically asked.

"Gary Mason's dead!" Michael said.

Ford looked up in surprise. "What? England's most handsome leading man is dead?"

"Exactly."

"What's happened? Any there any eyewitnesses?"

"Me – to a certain extent..."

Ford looked at him. "Wow," he said, "this is sensational! And you look as if you've got a dead dog in your pocket."

Michael threw an envelope on the table

"Here are photos of his dead body," he said, "to choose from."

"Start writing this up right away. And let Ben know. After all, it's his speciality."

When Michael had told the crime reporter Ben Dickens everything about what had happened, the little man just nodded. It looked like he was waiting to hear this. But that couldn't be the case. There was no way that could be.

Michael wanted to go to his desk and start writing up the story but Ben held him back with a wave of his hand. "Do you have much on right now?"

Michael shook his head. "No. Why?"

"Do you want to stand in for me for two weeks from tomorrow? I have to go away. A sudden, urgent, family affair..."

The next morning, Michael found his report on the front page of the *Comet*. He read it again during breakfast and was almost satisfied with himself. The phone rang. He put the newspaper away and lifted the receiver.

"It's Karin Lund," said a dark voice at the other end of the line. "I would like to thank you."

"What for?"

"I have read your article in the newspaper. And you haven't said anything about our – our conversation ..."

"That wouldn't have looked good."

"Not for me. That's why I thank you."

"Oh, let's forget it. Are you calling from the studio?"

"No, filming has been cancelled at least until Tuesday."

"Fine. Can we meet for lunch?"

"Today?"

"Why not? At one o'clock in Pinellio's restaurant?"

Karin hesitated for a moment. Then she accepted Michael's invitation.

Michael's first meeting with Karin Lund was not a pure pleasure for him. He had to admit to himself that it was his fault.

He had expected too much. He had hoped she would confide in him. He didn't dare to ask her questions directly. When he cautiously tried to steer the conversation to the murder, he had no success. As much bait as he laid out, she just didn't bite. She acted as if she knew what he was thinking. It was certainly not due to the quality of the food in the Pinellio restaurant that he didn't like his meal. Karin ate with a great appetite. He admired how she wrapped the

93

spaghetti around her fork with a steady hand and fed it to her mouth. She behaved as if food was the most important thing in the world.

They drank a bottle of chianti together until it was empty, chatted and smiled at each other. Outwardly, this meeting was no different from the encounters Michael had had privately or professionally with other female celebrities from the film world. He drank the wine without tasting its flavour. It was the first time he had been with a woman that a man had tried to murder. Because it was clear to Michael that the murderer was after her and not Gary Mason. And she acted as if murder was the most commonplace thing in the world. No more remarkable than catching measles.

She only told him that she had rented a small flat in Notting Hill Gate for six months. With the progress of this film up in the air right now she didn't know what her plans were.

"I'd rather stay here in London and watch television. But who knows if I'll get more work?"

He toasted her future with her. And always had to remember that she might never experience this future. It was like being in a bad dream.

As they said goodbye, she promised to call him.


The next two days passed without Michael hearing from Karin Lund. Nothing else happened. Neither in his nor in Ben Dickens' work area.

Michael called Inspector Parker a few times. But the Scotland Yard man had to admit that he still hadn't discovered any leads.

"It's bizarre!" snorted Parker on the phone. "If I think about it correctly, all we know is that someone fired a gun and Gary Mason was hit..."

On the third day, Michael called Karin Lund to invite her to the premiere of a musical. No one answered the phone.

Reluctantly, he went to the theatre alone in the evening. After only half an hour, he regretted it. The music was bland, the plot thin, the actors were mediocre.

Boredom drove him to the theatre bar during the break. Around him, the usual premiere audience chatted. Big evening dresses, diamonds, real and fake elegance next to each other – it was always like this on such evenings.

Michael sat down at the bar and disconsolately drank a gin with tonic.

Then he saw her. And she was not alone. She stood at the other end of the bar. He first recognised her by her long blonde hair. It fell loosely down her back and glittered in the glow of the lighting. She was wearing a dark blue evening dress. The man she spoke to was wearing a tuxedo with a shawl collar and velvet cuffs. Michael didn't like the look of him. He was medium-sized, dark and the narrow beard over his upper lip seemed to be drawn with ink. Probably a foreigner, Michael thought. He caught himself staring at the man. And it took him a few minutes to realise that he was jealous.

He resisted this feeling. He had seen Karin Lund twice, and nothing gave him the right to be jealous. What did he know about her, except that she was beautiful, he liked her, and she was involved in some dark affair?

Maybe the man was her agent. Or the representative of a foreign film company.

Michael wondered if he should go and talk to her. Then the bell for the second act rang. The interval was over.

The two got up and approached him. Now Karin had to see him. She had her head tilted to the side and listened to the words of her companion.

When they were by his side, she suddenly looked up. Looked right into his eyes. He was waiting for the smile that surely had to come. But she turned her head away indifferently and continued to talk to the other man, in a language that Michael didn't understand.

He looked after them until they disappeared back into the auditorium. Then he turned around with a jerk and emptied his glass. The incident worried him so much that he had the greatest trouble concentrating on the final act of the play. What was going on with Karin Lund? She had cut him dead. Deliberately overlooked him, as if he was her worst enemy.

When he was lying in bed and trying in vain to fall asleep, Karin's behaviour was still going around in his head. Did it have anything to do with the man she was with? Eventually, he fell into a restless sleep and dreamed that Karin called him day and night and that he refused to answer her calls.

Suddenly, he was startled. The phone was ringing. He looked at his wristwatch. It was four thirty in the morning. He picked up the phone and immediately recognised the Scottish brogue of the paper's night editor.

"They left your number and said that you were temporarily responsible for all major criminal cases."

"That's right," Michael admitted sleepily.

"Then off you go to Ronway Mansions, boy. On the Bayswater Road."

"What's going on?"

"Someone has been killed. That's all I know. Ring me when you know what's happened and have got some copy for me. For the early edition. But be quick!"

Ten minutes later, Michael was in the block of flats on the Bayswater Road. On the first floor, he saw a small group of police officers and reporters through an open apartment door.

He recognised a colleague from the *Mirror* among all the strange faces.

"Hi, Joe. What's going on?"

"Hello, Michael! What are you doing here?"

"I'm covering for Ben. He's on holiday. Who's been killed?"

"A woman. Nobody knows her name yet. I'm not sure they'll ever find out who it was. She was stabbed to death."

"Didn't she live here?"

"No. The caretaker claims that he has never seen her before."

"Who's flat is it?"

"Someone called Eric Shroeman or something like that. He does a lot of business in Holland apparently. He might even be Dutch. The caretaker doesn't know exactly. Anyway, he's currently in Holland."

"And who discovered the murder?"

"The caretaker heard the woman screaming. He immediately called the police. They broke down the door. But she was already dead. The murderer must have escaped via the fire escape."

"Thanks, Joe!"

"No problem. By the way, the photographers seem to be finished. The forensics have already gone. They'll take out the body pretty soon. If you still want to see it. It might be good for your report ..."

"Thanks for the tip, Joe."

Michael went to Inspector Philips.

"I'm Michael Collins from the *Comet*. I'm here instead of Ben Dickens."

"Philips." The Inspector shook his hand. "Is Ben sick?"

"He's on holiday," Michael explained. He nodded his head towards the door. "Can I take a quick look at the body?"

"If you want," Philips said. "But be quick. She'll be taken away fairly soon. The ambulance is already here."

Michael stepped into the brightly furnished bedroom. The body lay on the wide double bed. The long light blonde hair hung tangled around the narrow head. There was a stain on the blue evening dress. Big. Dark. Damp...

He saw the wound made by the murder weapon. Someone had pushed a pointed object into her chest. Right into the heart.

It was not a pretty sight. Michael opened his mouth, but his voice failed. He swallowed a few times.

"Inspector," he shouted hoarsely.

"What is it?" Philips was next to him in a moment.

"Call Inspector Parker," Michael said tonelessly. "This is his case."

"Why? Do you know the girl?"

Michael straightened up. His eyes burned.

"Yes," he said slowly. "She's called :.."

He swallowed hard again.

"Her name is Karin Lund."

# EPISODE TWO

Inspector Philips looked at the excited reporter in surprise. "Are you sure that the stabbed woman's name is Karin Lund?" he asked.

Michael Collins nodded. "Yes. She's a young film actress. From Sweden. A few days ago, she was shot at. At the Commodore Film Studios. Tom Parker's in charge of the case."

He didn't pay attention to the instructions the Inspector was giving. He was still looking at the murdered woman. Who could have done this to the beautiful girl with such hatred? An irrepressible anger at the murderer rose inside him. Was it the man from the theatre bar?

Someone put a hand on his shoulder. "Come on!" said his colleague from the *Mirror*. "I know it's tough the first time, but you've got a report to phone in."

When Detective Inspector Parker arrived, Michael had just finished on the phone. Parker was briefed, started the search for the owner of the flat and went to have breakfast with his friend.

"I think you've got a lot to tell me," he said as steaming cups of tea stood in front of them.

Michael Collins let his gaze wander round the long restaurant. At small tables, early risers and late-stayers with tired faces ate their sandwiches.

"Yes, Tom," Michael admitted, "I do have something to tell you." He told Tom all about Karin's strange request after the attack at the film studios not to call the police. Of his suspicion that she was concealing something from him.

"I can't prove it, of course" he continued. "But I'm convinced that the attack wasn't aimed at Gary Mason, but at Karin Lund herself. And she knew why she was being shot at. She was afraid. But it was strange. I couldn't get rid of the feeling that she wasn't as afraid of the murderer as she was of something else – some secret or other being discovered."

Tom Parker looked at him thoughtfully, "So you mean Gary Mason wasn't the intended target? That him being shot was an accident?"

"I think so, but of course I can't be sure. In any case, the deaths of Gary Mason and Karin Lund seem to be directly linked and should therefore be investigated together."

"So, with Karin Lund you had the impression that she was hiding something."

"If you want to call it that, yes," Michael replied. "There seemed to be something she was more afraid of than the murderer."

"And you have no idea what that was?"

"No, but since she's only been in England for a very short time, it must have to do with her past. In Sweden."

He talked about their lunch together and the strange encounter in the theatre bar.

"I'm guessing the man she was with must be the murderer," he concluded.

Tom shook his head with a smile. "I understand your enthusiasm as well as your hatred of the murderer. But believe an old practitioner: It's never really as easy as it looks to you now."

But he did admit that the stranger was suspicious. "Of course we'll do everything we can to find him. But don't be surprised if he's a complete red herring in the end!"

Michael pushed his empty plate aside. "There's something else," he said insistently. "The man she was with talked to Karin in a foreign language. I couldn't tell what it was, it may have been Swedish. Or maybe Dutch."

"You mean your stranger from the bar could be this man Schroeman whose flat it is ..."

"Exactly. Isn't that a line of inquiry you could pursue?"

"I'll try," sighed the inspector.

Eighteen cigarette butts lay in his ashtray when Michael finished the detailed report for the late edition. He tore the last piece of paper out of the typewriter and ran his eyes over it again. Then he got up and walked between desks to Arthur Ford, the editor.

"Finished?" he asked, taking the manuscript out of Michael's hand. "How many pages? Six? Any bright ideas for the headline?"

Michael shook his head. Before he could say anything, one of Arthur's phones rang.

"Ford," his boss said. "What? Oh, that old cheese. We don't want to run anything about that again. I said no and that's an end to it." He replaced the phone. "By the way," he turned to Michael, "do you know that Ben has been seen in town? He –"

This time it was the other phone ringing. While he lifted the second receiver, the first one rang again. "Ford," he said, into the receiver and ordered Michael with a head movement to answer the other phone. He wrote down an address, then shouted a name into the room and gave the note to a young man approaching in a hurry.

"Who was it?" he asked Michael.

"You're needed upstairs. Urgently."

"I was expecting that. What I wanted to say: Ben is obviously hanging out in the city. I guess..."

He got up and went to the door. Michael was left with nothing left to do than to walk with him. "I suspect," said the editor "that Ben is on the trail of some big deal. He did this a few years ago. Took a holiday so that no one knew what he was up to and then came in with a big scoop. See you!"

The lift doors closed quickly behind him.

101

Although Michael was constantly in contact with Parker over the next two days, he didn't learn anything new. He spent an entire morning at the Yard, looking through hundreds of photos. But none of the men whose photographs he looked at were the stranger from the bar. He hesitated over two or three pictures. Perhaps a certain similarity? But then he put them back shaking his head. He was almost certain: the bony face of the man who was last seen with Karin Lund wasn't there.

This work left him little time to think. His film column had to be finished, in addition to Ben Dickens' work, who he was standing in for. And on top of that, Arthur Ford also had a job for him at the weekend.

"Watch the new panel game they're showing on tv tomorrow night."

"That one about people's places of birth?"

"Yes. *Where Do I Come From*? I want thirty lines of general criticism about it, ok?"

Sunday afternoon was humid and foggy. Michael was not sorry that the television assignment took away his desire to go out. He called Tom Parker and invited him round for the evening. When his friend came, they drew the curtains and sat down with glasses of wine by the fireplace. The flames cast twitching shadows into the room as the men talked about the two murders.

Sometimes Tom looked anxiously into the face of his friend, whose eyes seemed to be embedded even deeper in shadows in this lighting than during the day. What a contrast to the Michael he had known in Oxford and even later: he had been sporty, broad-shouldered, tall, with short dark hair and a warm, contagious laugh. Now he sat bent over, his chin resting in his hand, staring into the fire. As if he could find there the solution to what was turning over in his head.

Karin Lund, of course! It must have been love at first sight. Why else would Michael's behaviour have changed so much in just a few days? No. There could only be one reason: the death of the beautiful Swedish woman.

"It's eight o'clock," Tom finally reminded Michael who got up and turned on the television. Then they turned their chairs round and waited for the show to start.

It was as always: the continuity announcer said what the next programme was, followed by the opening credits and then the quizmaster introduced the new panel game and the team who would be playing it before the camera panned over to show the densely packed audience.

The quizmaster explained the game.

"Ladies and gentlemen, here in this basket I have the torn off sections of your tickets. My lovely assistant," he smiled at a long-legged creature hovering on the stage behind him, "will reach into the basket with her eyes closed. She will pull out a ticket and then give it to me and I'll say the row and number of the seat printed on it. Then we will ask the audience member sitting in that seat to come up on to the stage to join us. The two ladies and the three gentlemen of the panel are allowed to ask them questions that can only be answered with "yes" or "no". If the team guesses the birthplace of the challenger before the tenth question, then he is honourably defeated and receives a bronze plaque in gratitude for his cooperation. If he succeeds in answering "no" ten times, then he is the winner and receives the large silver winner's plaque." He held up a bright disc the size of a saucer and turned it on all sides.

"I'll explain all the rest of the rules as and when I need to. Ah – one more thing: Challengers born in London would offer our five panel members an all-too-easy game. For them, therefore, in addition to the city, the district must also be guessed. – And so now on to the BBC's new panel game! On to *Where Do I Come From?*! Can we have the first challenger, please!"

The camera watched close-up as the first ticket stub was pulled out of the basket.

"Row four, seat number seventeen," the quizmaster announced.

Another camera panned into the audience, slid along the fourth row and finally zoomed in to the face of a young, pretty woman.

"Would you be kind enough to be our first challenger this evening for our panel?" the quizmaster asked.

She looked to the left, where apparently her boyfriend or husband was sitting. He nodded encouragingly at her. Then she stood up, still a little hesitant, pushed her way along the row and then becoming more self-confident, walked down the middle aisle of the audience to the stage.

"Thank you very much for coming up – and good luck with our little game," the quizmaster welcomed her. He asked her to sit down, had her write her birthplace on a piece of paper and passed it on to his assistant. Seconds later, invisible to the panel, the name Hamburg appeared on an illuminated board. Friendly applause echoed in the studio. Luckily, the audience seemed to think, a tourist! That will be hard to guess.

"Born in London?" asked the first panel member.

"No," the answer came in accent-free English.

"A no, so there are still nine open," registered the quizmaster.

"In England?" came the second question from one participant.

"No."

"Two away, eight more," said the quizmaster.

"In Europe?" asked the third.

"Yes..."

"On the continent?" probed number three.

"Yes..."

"West of the Rhine?" he added.

"No."

The audience murmured contentedly. This was a balanced fight in which both parties had chances. But they were wrong.

The next question was a shot in the dark.

"In Germany?"

"Yes..."

"North of the Main?"

"Yes," came the answer.

After that, it was easy.

The second challenger, an Englishman from Blackpool, they solved after only three questions.

Then came the "Mystery Challenger", a man with a selected unusual birthplace. For the first broadcast, the BBC had discovered a man who had been born on a passenger steamer between Liverpool and New York. The camera panned into the audience and captured rows of smiling faces when the television monitors that only the audience and viewers at home could see announced this. But the panel was warned by the laughter. It tapped on plane, camel caravan or ship from the outset and solved the task with an ease that promised little excitement for the rest of the broadcast.

"There's no way this programme's going to take off. It wouldn't take you more than five questions to guess any of their places of birth. They can't just randomly pluck people out of the audience. They're going to have to choose the challengers in advance if ..."

He broke off and stared at the screen, where the camera was showing a close-up of the man whose ticket stub had been picked next and therefore was going to be the next challenger.

"What is it?" Tom Parker couldn't see anything special about the man on the television screen.

"That man! That's the man from the bar! He's the man I saw with Karin Lund!" Excitedly, Michael jumped up. "Come on, we have to do something!"

His friend pushed him back into his armchair. "Calm down, Michael! Calm down. Don't get over excited. You've got this man on your brain. Now you're imagining seeing him everywhere."

"No, that's him! It really is," Michael protested.

"Take a proper look at him first," Tom said calmly. "Then we'll see if it's him."

The man on the screen stood up. He approached the camera calmly and confidently. The studio lights on his face became brighter. The cheek bones could be seen more and more clearly, the chin, the almost angular bridge of the nose.

"That's him! I'm sure of it!" Michael implored his friend. But Tom only raised his hand in warning.

"Let's hear him speak first. That'll help us make up our minds. If he's a foreigner, then I'll take your word for it. If not..." He didn't say anything else. But Michael knew what he meant. Tom apparently thought he was mad. Michael forced himself to sit still. The proof had to come soon. The first yes or no had to betray the stranger.

"Born in Great Britain?" was the first question.

"Yes," replied the stranger loud and clear.

Michael held his breath.

"In London?" came the next question.

Michael no longer listened to the words being said. Only on their sound. Could this be the same man he saw in the bar with Karin that night? Who he had thought was a foreigner? The next question was not precise enough.

"I can't answer that with yes or no," the stranger fended off. "Would you mind rephrasing it?"

His English sounded fluent and pure. He made his statements confidently and without thinking.

The panel had trouble with him. At the tenth no, it had only placed him in the county of Cornwall. They still hadn't found his birthplace.

The quizmaster approached him and congratulated him on being the first winner of the new game. "Where do you really come from, if I may ask?"

"From Fowey," said the stranger. A roaring whisper spread throughout the audience and a swell of warm applause followed for the winner.

The quizmaster clapped along, then stepped back up to the microphone and said, "May I ask you for your name?"

"Vorse, Victor Vorse," was the answer.

"Victor Vorse? Mr. Vorse, could it be that I've read your name somewhere before – or maybe even heard it on tv?"

Vorse nodded. "I was British amateur dancing champion in 1955. More precisely, the British amateur waltz champion. The event was broadcast by the BBC so that's probably it."

Once again, the applause sounded. Then Vorse left the stage, his silver plaque in hand. The camera followed him.

When he sat down in his seat again, a dark-haired lady sitting next to him congratulated him. She was elegant and very well dressed.

"I'm still sure that's him," Michael said. "Can't we do anything, Tom?"

"What?" the Inspector asked back. "Even if he is the man you're talking about, it's not a crime to go to the theatre with a woman who is later murdered"

"Can't we go there and talk to him?"

"By the time we get through the fog, the studio will have long cleared out. No, Michael, I think you'd better leave this to me. I'll get his address from the tv people. They must keep a record of some sort. Sometimes things crop up afterwards and they might want to get in touch with him. I also think that if he's your man, it's better that he doesn't see you."

The game on television went on for a while, but Vorse remained the only successful challenger.

When Parker left, Michael sat down at his typewriter and tried to write his story but he struggled to focus on that.

How did Victor Vorse get onto this tv show? Did that mean anything? Would a murderer even dare to show his face to ten million viewers?

The next morning, Victor Vorse's photo was in the *Daily Pictorial*. Five million readers saw it and read underneath: "The man who beat the panel."

Tom Parker phoned Michael at the paper's office. He had news. Could they meet for dinner?

Shortly after half past one, Michael left the *Comet* building and went to a pub near Whitehall. Tom Parker was standing at the bar and was drinking a pint of beer. He ordered two more. Then, glasses in hand, they went into the oak-panelled dining room and sat down at a corner table.

"I talked to your Mr. Vorse," Parker said with a smile.

"You've been to Cornwall?"

"Of course not. You fool. He was only born there."

"That's what he says!"

"I got his address from the people at the BBC. He lives here in London. In Ealing. He owns a dance school. His assistant's name is Connie Halliday and she sat next to him in the studio last night."

"The dark haired one?"

The detective nodded. "That's right. Well, the two of them wanted to go out last night and by chance ended up going to the show at the television studios. They didn't want to go far because of the fog, says Vorse."

"That may be so. In any case, I've had a really good look at the photos of him in the papers now. I'm still convinced he's the man from the bar."

108

"You're right. But the fact that he nevertheless appeared on television indicates his innocence."

"I'm not so sure," Michael said. "Perhaps he's just thinks that no one saw him when he was in the theatre with Karin."

"He says he'd never met Miss Lund let alone go to the theatre with her," Parker said matter-of-factly. "He answered all my questions openly, of course I've had his past checked. But as far as we know so far, there is nothing against him."

During the meal, Michael asked, "Is there anything new on Eric Schroeman?"

"Nothing. If he flew to Holland, as the caretaker – his name is Bert Howard, by the way – claims, then he has disappeared completely from sight."

"Has the caretaker been able to say if Karin ever visited this Schroeman?"

"He claims he's never seen her before. He also alleges he hasn't seen anyone go into the flat since Schroeman left. He believes that Miss Lund and her murderer both must have entered the flat via the fire escape."

Michael put down his cutlery and wiped his mouth with a napkin.

"I don't know what you think of it, Tom," he finally said, "but it seems pretty sure to me that someone is lying like the devil about all this."

"That's usually the case," grinned the detective.

When Michael returned to his office, the editor looked even more worried than usual.

"Go to Ben's desk," he said. "Look through it. Try to figure out what Ben was working on and where he is now."

"What's up?"

"I've just had a call. From his wife. He didn't come home last night. For the first time in years. She's worried. Okay?"

Michael whistled quietly between his teeth. It couldn't be

heard with the noise made by the typewriters and telephones. Then he nodded and went to Ben's desk.

Cards were pinned to the wall behind the desk. A map of the police divisions in London and a list of the police stations in each of them, a map of the River Thames, a larger map of the city centre with mysteriously scribbled marks. Dickens had written his articles here for many years. Factual, sober-sounding articles. About London's underworld and their activities.

Michael saw that the shabby little desk had stacks of newspaper clippings, index cards and so on. Notes and photos covered it. Shrugging his shoulders, he set to work.

First of all he looked through all the handwritten notes. Ben's handwriting was hard to read – like the man himself perhaps? Then he started to look through the rest. What a mess! What's that? A receipt? No idea what it was for. Had anything happened to Ben? Why hadn't he gone home last night? Had he and his wife had a row? No, if so then she wouldn't be – wait! What was that? A brochure. From a dance school.

Stop! Don't miss anything! What was the name of the school? The School of Ballroom Dancing. It meant nothing to him.

But hold on! The address! Lansdale Grove, Ealing. And later on, in smaller print: "Dance instructors on the courses: Connie Halliday and Victor Vorse".

# EPISODE THREE

Michael Collins leaned back and lit a cigarette. Think! Forget the noise of the editorial staff running around at full speed. Focus on the crucial question: How did the brochure of the Victor Vorse Dance School end up on Ben Dickens' desk?

His missing colleague Ben had often claimed that he knew London's underworld better than Scotland Yard. Had he been watching Vorse? Had he known something about him? Had he believed he had committed a crime?

Michael pulled Ben's rickety typewriter towards him and typed:

1. Attempted murder of Karin Lund (or murder of Gary Mason?).

2. I tell Ben about it. He immediately takes a holiday. The boss says it's because he is on the trail of something big.

3. I see Vorse in the theatre bar with Karin.

4. A few hours later, Karin is stabbed to death.

5. Vorse denies any acquaintance with Karin.

6. Ben's wife calls: her husband has gone missing.

7. I find the brochure of Victor Vorse's Dance School on Ben's desk.

Michael picked up the brochure again. It was a thin booklet – hardly more than a pamphlet. In one corner was a picture of Victor Vorse. "Winner of the Amateur Dance Tournament 1955" was written underneath.

Should he call Tom Parker? No, the Inspector would only put on that superior smile of his again and say that experience has shown him that such simple coincidences often mean nothing.

He picked up the phone and dialled the number that was on the dance school brochure.

A woman's voice answered. She sounded a bit too polite. Especially when he said he was interested in a one-to-one course.

"When do you want to start?" the voice asked.

"As soon as possible."

"We have a cancellation for tonight. If it suits you, you can come at 7:30 p.m."

"Yes, that suits me."

"Fine. Your name, please."

He said his name. Then he asked, "I assume that Miss Connie Halliday will be my dance teacher?"

"That's right," came the answer. "I'm Miss Halliday. I'll be waiting for you at 7:30 p.m."

Michael walked down the corridor to the typing pool. There he spoke with an elderly secretary whom he knew had occasionally done some work for Ben Dickens.

"Does this booklet mean anything to you?" he asked, showing her the brochure. "It was on Ben's desk."

She slowly leafed through the booklet. Then she shook her head.

"He never talked to me about it," she said sadly.

Michael parked his car in a side street and first looked at the building. Mr Vorse's Dance School had been built in a modern style, with large windows and an elegantly curved canopy over the entrance.

He rang the bell. The door opened and the sound of dance music came floating out. A woman stood in front of him.

He immediately recognised her as being Connie Halliday. The television camera had shown her and Victor Vorse very clearly. She seemed a little older close-up. Certain hard lines around the eyes and around the mouth told him that she knew life hadn't only got its friendly sides.

She led him into a room that was empty except for a record player and a few chairs. While she was putting on a new record, she asked him how he had heard about the school.

"I read your brochure," he said, "and then I remembered it when I saw you and Mr. Vorse on tv."

She nodded and smiled. "Wasn't that a good advertisement? – So, let's get started. First I'll show you a Madison solo..."

He had to admit that she cut an excellent figure. Her movements were smooth and seemed anything but rehearsed. The coquettish glances she threw at him in between were in strange contrast to the sober explanations she made about the individual steps.

Then they both danced together. Michael quickly had his right foot pointing out. It wasn't as easy as it looked.

They tried again and talked about the television show in between. But as skilfully as he tried to direct the conversation, he couldn't manage to bring it round so that they talked about Victor Vorse. As her hand was on his arm, he said, "Have you heard of this terrible murder of Karin Lund?"

He felt her hand stiffen. But in the next moment she was completely relaxed again.

"No," she said emphatically yet carelessly. "I haven't read a newspaper or listened to a radio in the last few days. Who is Karin Lund?"

"A young Swede. A young film actress, she's been stabbed to death..."

At that moment, the door opened. A man came in. That man was Victor Vorse.

"Good evening," he said politely. "Will you allow me to kidnap Miss Halliday from you for a moment?"

He pulled the dance teacher aside and talked to her quietly for a few minutes. This gave Michael the opportunity to look at him closely. If he hadn't been one hundred percent sure before – now there was no doubt: this was the man he had seen in the theatre bar together with Karin Lund.

Seemingly indifferent, Michael went to the window and pretended to look out. He listened intently to every sound behind his back. When Vorse approached him, he could see him in the reflection on the windowpane.

What now?

If Vorse was armed, there was no point in a fight.

So should he escape?

Yes. The window was on ground level. Outside it was almost dark. A few steps, then he would be safely away.

"Mister Collins!"

As casually as he could, he turned around.

Vorse turned and stood at the door. He held the handle in his hand and bowed slightly in Michael's direction.

"Please excuse the disturbance. Miss Halliday is now available to you again."

Vorse smiled. But it was only his mouth that warmed. The eyes remained cold.


On the way home, Michael stopped next to a newspaper seller. He bought an evening newspaper and looked through the headlines in the glow of the interior lighting of his car.

On page five he found a short report about the new television programme. A hundred lines of text, plus a picture of Victor Vorse and the caption "The man who beat the panel". As he looked at the picture, a thought suddenly came to him: How about a visit to Bayswater Road?

Bert Howard, the caretaker, sat in the porter's box. He recognised Michael immediately.

"You were here with the police, weren't you?"

Michael nodded and offered Howard a cigarette. "From the *Evening Comet*."

"Weren't you the one who recognised Miss Lund?"

"I'd met her at the studios. During filming."

"Oh, and that's why you're interested in the case?"

"A little. That's what my job's all about. Have you heard anything from your tenant, this Mr. Shroeman?"

"Nothing at all, sir. If you ask me, I find the whole thing extremely strange."

"Mysterious do you mean? That's usually the case with murders." He pulled the newspaper out of his pocket, opened it and pointed to Victor Vorse's picture.

"Has this man ever visited Eric Shroeman?"

Howard seemed hesitant. But then he shook his head violently. "I saw the man on tv yesterday. If I knew him as an acquaintance of Mr. Shroeman, I would have called the police immediately."

Michael nodded and said goodbye. He wasn't at all sure that the caretaker had told him the truth. But there was no point in prolonging an unproductive conversation.

Shortly after ten o'clock he was in his flat. He started to run himself a hot bath. Due to the noise of the water, he almost didn't hear the phone ring. At first, he didn't recognise the voice on the other end. Then he suddenly realised that he was talking to Connie Halliday.

"How much do you care about Karin Lund, Mr Collins?"

"A lot," Michael said calmly.

"That's what I thought."

"So you know who she was?"

"I couldn't speak before. Someone could have overheard us. But if you want, we can meet somewhere else."

"Tonight?"

"Why not?"

"Somewhere in town?"

"Yes. I know a small restaurant in Soho. The Osteria. We can sit there and not be disturbed. It's on Melkin Street. Just off Poland Street. Can you be there by eleven o'clock?"

"Eleven it is!" he said and hung up the phone.

He returned to the bathroom and turned off the taps. Then he went into the living room and poured himself three fingers of whisky. He wondered whether he should call Tom Parker.

Actually, it was his duty to do so. But if the woman had turned to him and not to the police, then she must have a reason for it. Perhaps she was so deeply involved in the matter that she was afraid of Scotland Yard?

If this assumption was correct, then she would remain silent when he came with the Inspector.

He drank the whisky. No, he had to go through with this meeting alone. He could still tell Tom if something tangible came out of it.

He took the lift down and went to his car. As he sat behind the wheel, he pulled a city map out of the glove compartment. He found Poland Street straight away.

A quarter of an hour later he was there. Parking was prohibited on Melkin Street so he parked the car on the main street and continued on foot.

A light breeze rustled with the scraps of paper in the gutter as he walked along the narrow one-way street. It looked like a ravine between the tall houses. It had no pavement and just had room for a car. He thought it strange that no illuminated sign pointed to a restaurant. Maybe it was a basement restaurant? They often didn't have a protruding advertising sign. But even then, he should have seen the reflection of some illuminated lettering.

An eerie feeling crept up on him. Was this a trap?

He looked at his watch. Three minutes to eleven.

Michael gave himself a jolt and walked on. Involuntarily, he listened to see if steps were following him. But everything was quiet.

Suddenly, he heard the soft hum of an engine. He looked around. A car had turned into the street. With dimmed headlights, it drove behind him at walking pace.

Michael walked faster. The narrow alley between the gloomy threatening buildings offered no room to avoid the vehicle. He'd be hopelessly trapped between the fender and the wall of one of the buildings. Apparently, the driver was a very reasonable man. He patiently drove after Michael, incredibly patient! Like a ready to jump predator in the jungle. Determined.

The reporter quickened his steps. He thought desperately. It was almost a hundred yards to the next corner. Should he run? The guy behind him wouldn't shoot. The bang would startle the whole street.

Eighty more yards. If that was the murderer behind him, then he would knock him down from behind. Then turn off his lights and drive out of the alley.

Seventy yards left. Should he run? Would his lead be enough?

At that moment, the headlights flashed. The engine behind him howled.

Michael sped off. The shadow of his own legs danced in front of him. Faster! Don't turn around! Faster!

In the first few seconds he had gained ground. But the pursuer caught up.

Thirty more yards maybe! Faster, for God's sake!

Too late! The car was close behind him. Every moment...

There – on the right! A dark opening! At the last second, Michael threw himself into the open doorway of a small shop. The pursuer raced past. For seconds, Michael lay crouching on the stone floor. Then he picked himself up and felt his way back to the door, which stood out only slightly from the darkness of the stop. Blood throbbed in his temples as he carefully peered along the alley on both sides. There was nothing to see.

He leaned against the doorpost and felt for cigarettes in his pockets. He found the full pack he had put in at home, tore it open and pulled out a cigarette.

"Do you need a light?" asked a voice behind him.

He turned around. A shadow came out of the background and walked towards him.

Then a lighter flared up. In his glow, he saw the wrinkled face of an old man.

"I wanted to..." he stuttered. "Excuse me..."

"It's ok," hummed the old man. "Light your cigarette!"

Michael did.

"Thank you," he said. "I still have to apologise for falling into your shop."

"It doesn't matter," said the old man. "I saw what happened. Was the guy drunk?"

"Must have been," Michael replied.

"I was about to go home," said the old man. "I've been working late. Doing returns for the tax office – you know the sort of thing. If you trade in antiques like I do..."

"So you had just turned off the lights?" interrupted Michael.

"I had opened the door so that the cigarette smoke could get out. I had already turned off the light. In two minutes, the shop would have been closed and locked up for the night."

"Well, I was lucky," said Michael. He looked down the street again. "The guy seems to be gone now. I won't keep you any longer. Thank you very much."

He didn't wait to hear what the old man answered. He walked quickly the few yards to the next corner. There he stopped in amazement.

There was a restaurant on the corner. The densely shrouded windows hardly let light penetrate the street. That's why he hadn't seen it earlier. But now he clearly recognised the name on the window: Tony's Osteria.

On the spur of the moment, he pushed the door open and went in. It was an Italian restaurant. In any case, the restaurant owner had made an effort to give this simple London corner restaurant an Italian look. Pictures of Rome and Naples hung on the walls. Empty wine bottles with Italian labels hung on strings of braided straw.

Connie Halliday wasn't there. But he saw about three dozen other people. Some couples, a table with probably some real Italians, three or four unsociable beer drinkers and a group of people who looked like tourists

Michael sat down at a free table so that he could see the door. The waitress came. He ordered a whisky and looked at the pictures on the wall with great interest. Right next to him hung a still photo from a film. A radiant smiling man's face. Michael recognised it immediately. He also knew the name of the dedication: "My dear Tony! Gary Mason."

The whisky was brought. Michael tried to collect his thoughts. They had wanted to lure him into a trap, that was clear. They – that was Connie Halliday, wasn't it?

So he was on the right track? What else could it mean? No one would try to kill a harmless man.

Wasn't it time to notify Tom Parker? The Inspector would be annoyed with him anyway for not having told him in the first place.

But what could he tell him? Tom knew his suspicions about Vorse – and beyond that there was nothing new to tell. No proof of anything. Someone had tried to run him over. That's what he thought. He couldn't prove it.

And he didn't know who had been driving the car. How could he go to Tom and report for a second time something about a car whose licence plate he didn't know? Should he tell him that maybe Gary Mason wasn't just the innocent victim of a coincidence after all? That his photo in Tony's Osteria rather suggested that there was a mysterious connection between Gary's death and his own attempted murder? How was he supposed to explain all this to Tom? When his friend already thought he was exaggerating anyway?

No, he had to wait. He had to...

Michael had the unpleasant feeling that someone was watching him. He raised his head with a jerk and looked straight into the eyes of a man standing at the door looking at him through the crack of the curtains. Just for a moment. Then the face disappeared. The door slammed shut.

Michael jumped up. But then he heard a car driving away outside.

Slowly he sat back down in his chair. Without paying attention to the fact that a few people looked at him and what he was doing. He had only one thought: What had Ben Dickens been doing here? Why had he fled the moment he saw him? Why?

"Do you want to pay?" asked the waitress next to him, who had seen him get up and sit down again.

He paid and went out into the street. There was nothing to see. The narrow Melkin Street lay dark and silent in front of him. At the other end, the brighter Poland Street, where his car was parked, shone.

Should he walk back down the alley again? No, that was out of the question. It would have been criminally reckless.

A taxi drove by. Michael waved it down, got in and gave his address. He'd be able to collect his car tomorrow. And he would take a close look at it before he drove off in it. The murderer was versatile in his methods. Who'd know if he'd planted a bomb under it...?

He shook his head. Was he really beginning to see things that weren't there?

The taxi curved around a parked car and stopped in front of his house. "Three shillings and six pence, sir," said the driver.

Michael paid and got out. The car door slammed shut behind him. He watched the taxi go until it disappeared around the next street corner.

Then he turned around and walked towards the bright glass door of his house. But he stopped. Something was wrong.

Someone was sitting in a parked car. He had seen him clearly when he turned around. Michael put his hand quietly into his pocket and pulled out his keys. His movements were angular like those of a robot. But he took a step further although he knew that he would make an ideal target in front of the glass pane.

A desperate determination had taken possession of him. The determination of a man who wanted to know whether he was a fantasising coward or not. And when it came to his life, he couldn't run away.

He had to go through with it. He had to overcome his fear!

His nerves were tense as he raised his hand with the key in it. Now he was standing right in front of the glass illuminated from the inside. Now...

Then a shot rang out from behind him. One more – and a third. The window shattered.

With a gurgling scream, Michael collapsed.

# EPISODE FOUR

Michael Collins lay on the street, hoping he looked dead enough. He hoped the murderer wouldn't shoot again if he...

The beam of a flashlight hit him. Michael didn't move a millimetre. Not even when the light wandered over his dislocated body.

Out of the corner of his eye, he saw that the bluish shimmering barrel of a pistol appeared next to the lamp.

The murderer aimed.

Michael gritted his teeth.

A window opened above him. "What kind of noise is that?" roared the deep voice of one of the residents. "Can't we even sleep in peace anymore? Where are we? In Cuba?"

The flashlight and pistol disappeared. While other windows lit up and doors opened, the dark, unlit car pulled away. Like a shadow, it disappeared around the next corner.

Michael got up and brushed the dust off his suit. Then he unlocked his door and quickly went into the house to avoid curious neighbours asking questions.

He went straight to the phone and dialled Tom Parker's private number.

"Listen, Tom," he explained to the sleepy replying friend, "I need you. Right away. It's about Karin Lund. Yes, I have something to tell you..."

"Of course he thought I was dead," Michael said. "I dropped to the ground as if I'd really been shot. My ribs still hurt from it."

It was a bright morning. They sat in Tom Parker's office, a friendly space you wouldn't expect in Scotland Yard's gloomy building.

"Are you sure you've told me everything now?" the Inspector asked.

Michael nodded emphatically. "Every word. Even every thought. Can you make any sense of it?"

"No."

"But it's all ..."

"What do you want me to say?" The Inspector leaned back and smiled indulgently. "My dear Michael, you are again jumping to hasty conclusions. Nothing is at all clear about the matter."

"But listen to me..."

"No, you listen to me. You don't know everything yet."

"What? Have you got something to tell me?"

"Yes. The doctors, during the post-mortem of Gary Mason's body, found that the movie star regularly – yes, what is it?"

A man in a white coat entered. He had a small cardboard box and an index card in his hand. "What is it, doctor?" the Inspector asked.

The man pulled the rimless glasses from his forehead and said, "I have here the bullets that were fired at Mr. Collins last night. You wanted to know if they came from the same gun that Gary Mason was shot with."

He put the box on the table and looked at the index card. "Unfortunately, I have to disappoint you, Inspector. The film actor was shot with a German Mauser pistol. The shots last night were fired from an American Smith & Wesson."

"Are you sure? Couldn't you have made a mistake?" asked Michael.

The man in the white coat adjusted his glasses again and looked at him. "Impossible," he replied. "Our tests are absolutely accurate."

Tom nodded affirmatively. "Thank you very much, doctor. Leave everything here."

He waited until the door had closed behind the departing doctor. Then he said, "You see, that changes the situation again."

"Sure," Michael interrupted him. "But you wanted to tell me what the doctors found when they examined Mason's body."

"Right – excuse the interruption. They have shown that Mason regularly injected himself with morphine."

"What?" Michael leaned forward tensely. "That would mean..."

"That may mean that he had dealings with drug dealers. That he himself was involved in drug smuggling. That..."

"... the shot may have been meant for him," Michael added. "It's odd that his picture's on the wall in the Osteria on Melkin Street, where I was almost killed by a hit and run. Tom, I believe we're on the right track!"

"And how do you explain that Karin Lund was also murdered?"

"Maybe she was also an addict?"

"No. In any case, the autopsy showed no signs of that."

"Hm, then..." Michael thought hard. "Then I don't know what to suggest."

Tom Parker smiled. "There's an old rule at the Yard: If you can't think of anything, then you have to do something!"

"Good!" Michael jumped up. "I suggest we drive to Melkin Street and take a closer look at this Tony who owns the place. If we go there in a police car then I can collect my car on the way back. It's still parked on Melkin Street."

The black-haired man behind the counter looked at him from big brown eyes.

"Yes, I'm Tony," he said in amazement. "What do you want with me?"

124

"Inspector Parker of Scotland Yard," Tom introduced himself. "I have a few questions. Mr..."

"Antonio Argento," said the restauranteur, wiping his hands on a clean cloth. "That's my name. But people always call me Tony. That's why I called the restaurant what I did."

He came around the counter.

"Please, gentlemen, why don't we take a seat?"

They sat down at a table that stood in front of one of the large windows.

"So, Mr. Argento," Tom began, "Gary Mason has been here many times, has he?"

"He was a regular customer of mine," Tony said. "He felt comfortable here. If he wasn't such a famous man, I would say: He was my friend."

"Who did he come with – the same people or …?"

Tony didn't answer. His eyes widened with fright. His mouth moved as if he wanted to say something. But he only uttered a groaning sound. Tom and Michael looked at him curiously.

Then the windowpane broke behind them. Something flew past, crashed into the counter and rolled back towards them!

"Get down!" shouted Tom. He jumped and pulled up the table so that the other two could throw themselves to the ground.

Michael and Tony understood immediately. In a flash, they both fell to the floor.

Then the hand grenade exploded!

The air pressure squeezed his lungs together. Michael closed his eyes. He thought he was suffocating. Finally – he could take his first breath. Cool, wonderfully fresh air that entered through the broken window behind him.

He straightened up slowly and saw how at the same moment Tom Parker raised his head.

In front of them lay Tony. His clothes were shredded. Michael bent down to him. Was it a shell splinter? The man had definitely been injured.

Michael ran to the phone.

"No, let me do that," Tom Parker shouted after him.

Michael stopped and left the phone to the Inspector.

"The boss, fast!" he heard Tom say. Then he turned to the door.

Just in time to notice a shadow moving behind the window frame.

"My God," he thought. "How stupid are we being! We're acting as if all the danger is over. In fact..."

He looked around for something to arm himself with. There – a splintered chair. With a jerk, he tore off a chair leg. Two or three quick steps, then he stood behind the door with the stick in both hands ready to hit.

Slowly the door opened. Tormenting, centimetre by centimetre. The shadow behind it moved.

Michael took a quick look over to the Inspector. He turned his back on him as he spoke on the telephone. "Send a doctor and an ambulance," Michael heard him say.

Then the door was pushed open with a jerk. Michael raised the chair leg then let it sink in amazement.

"Ben?" he asked hoarsely. "What are you doing here?"

Ben Dickens looked around the devastated restaurant.

Then he waved to the Inspector, who turned around.

"I was just about to ask you the same question," he said slowly. "I just happened to be passing by here ..."

"Like last night?" Michael interrupted him.

The little man looked at him from squinted eyes.

"You're too suspicious, old chap," he said calmly. "Why don't you leave the questions to Scotland Yard? Good day, Inspector."

"Good day, Dickens," replied Tom Parker, who was now off the phone. "You always did have a good nose for trouble. Even when you're on holiday you are right on the spot if something happens..."

Ben Dickens contorted his face to a polite smile. "Coincidence," he said.

The injured man moved, moaning.

"What's happened to Tony?" asked Dickens.

"Don't move him," said the Inspector. "He might have internal injuries. The doctor's on his way. How do you know him?"

"I eat here sometimes," replied the little man indifferently. "It has very passable cuisine. Doesn't look good for him right now, does it?"

"I'm not a doctor," the Inspector dodged the question. "Hang on, what's going on out there?"

Voices had become loud outside. "There's broken glass here," someone shouted. "It must have been here we heard the bang."

The door flew open. A policeman stood in front of them. When he saw the Inspector, he saluted.

"Can I do something for you, sir?"

"Thank you," Parker replied. "I've already been on to the Yard. Keep the door shut and those people out of here, that's all."

The uniformed man nodded, turned around, went out and closed the door behind him. Immediately afterwards, they heard him telling the people outside on the pavement to move on.

Again, the injured man moved. His mouth was warped

Michael went to him.

"Tom," he suddenly shouted. "I think he wants to say something!"

They knelt attentively next to Tony. His looked at the Inspector.

"What is it?" asked Parker insistently. "Tell us, Argento! Who threw that hand grenade? Why did they? Speak, man!"

Tony's chest rose and fell in a fast rhythm. He opened his lips. "Yes," he said slowly, "Yes... I... know..." He gasped with effort. "They... warn me... not to ...?"

"Not to speak to the police? But you can speak, Argento!" the Inspector assured him. "Who was it?"

"It was..." He hesitated. Restlessly, his eyes wandered from Tom to Michael. Then they seemed to stick to a point between them.

"Go on, Argento!" the Inspector urged. "Why are you hesitating? Tell me everything you know!"

The Italian didn't look at him. His eyes still looked rigidly over Parker's shoulder. "No," he said suddenly. "I know... nothing. I was...mistaken."

"But Tony!" Michael interfered. "You can't just say you know..." He broke off. It made no sense. The man didn't even listen. But where was he staring all the time? Michael followed the look of the injured man. As if under a compulsion, he turned around. And looked right into the little pinched eyes of Ben Dickens.

Tom Parker had also turned around. Mistrust was clearly on his face as he let his gaze wander from Dickens to Argento.

Then he reluctantly raised his head. Outside, cars braked. Doors were slammed shut. The room was filled with men. One of them, the police doctor, pushed his way through with a wave of his hand. "I'm sorry," the doctor growled, "but I have to spoil your fun." He then bent over the injured man and began to examine him.

Tom Parker spoke briefly with some of the newcomers. Then he pulled Michael aside. "Did you see it too?" he asked.

The reporter nodded. "He saw Ben Dickens. Suddenly he didn't want to speak anymore."

Parker pondered. "There is no point in interrogating Dickens now. We can't prove anything against him. He'll only deny everything."

"Maybe we can talk to Tony again later?" Michael suggested.

"We can try," said his friend.

They walked over. The doctor was in the process of examining Argento's legs.

"That looks like a good sign – he doesn't seem to be in so much pain now," Tom said quietly. "It doesn't look like he has any internal injuries."

They waited. The doctor carried on with his examination.

"Doctor!" Tom said to him.

"What do you want?" the physician asked unwillingly.

"Just one question: Is your patient capable of answering a few questions?"

The doctor attached the last bandage with skilful fingers. Then he stood up.

"No," he said dismissively. "This man has suffered a shock. He needs rest."

"When will he be ready?"

"It depends on how quickly he recovers. Maybe tomorrow. Maybe in a week. I'll let you know when it's okay to talk to him. Now please excuse me."

The doctor turned around and waved at two men who were standing ready with a stretcher.

"Wait," the Inspector stopped him. "Maybe you don't know: this is about solving the murders of Gary Mason and Karin Lund!"

The doctor folded his hands over his stomach. "Did he kill her?" he asked, nodding his head to Argento, who had just been laid on the stretcher. "No," said the Inspector. "But he..."

The doctor interrupted the Inspector by sending the bearers on their way with a nod of the head. "I'm sorry. Then you will have to wait until the poor devil is able to be questioned. Good day, gentlemen!"

They looked after him. Then they grinned at each other as if on command. "Ruddy doctor!" said Tom, "but I suppose he's only doing his job. Defending his patient like a lion's young."

"Sure," Michael admitted. "But what do we do now?"

Tom Parker was still grinning. "These hard-working gentlemen," he pointed out with a comprehensive hand gesture to several eagerly employed men in plain clothes, "are in the process of searching the restaurant. Others will question the whole neighbourhood outside to find out if anyone saw who threw the hand grenade or anyone who looked suspicious hanging around. One of them," he muffled his voice, "is ready outside in an unmarked car to follow Ben Dickens when he leaves."

"You're going to keep an eye on him?"

"As far as it can be done inconspicuously. I don't necessarily want to make myself look a fool by suspecting one of London's most respected crime reporters."

"You seem to know each other well enough."

"Yes, we do. That's why he moves here as freely as if he's one of us. He's been on the job for twenty-five years. Longer than most of the detectives here. He's never been guilty of anything. Never put a foot wrong. Only twice had a clash with the police, as far as I know. And the officials were wrong. My God, the man's almost a public institution."

"And yet you want him watched?"

Tom looked at him with a steely eye. "When it comes to murder, I have every suspect observed. Even if it were the Prime Minister of Great Britain. But now..."

"Sir," an excited voice interrupted him.

"Yes, Sergeant? What is it?"

"A syringe, sir! I thought..."

"What kind of syringe?" Tom walked towards the bar with long steps.

"Injection syringe, sir."

The sergeant held up the instrument. "And here, next to it, are ampoules. The drawer was closed. The injured man had the key in his pocket."

Tom leaned over the bar. "Don't touch anything. We need the fingerprints. Can you see what's on the ampoules?"

"No, but on the box," he twisted his head to see the writing more closely, and then straightened up with a jerk. "Morphine, sir!" he reported matter-of-factly. Michael whistled quietly through his teeth. Gary Mason had injected morphine. He was also a regular guest at the Ostaria. Tony, the owner, was his friend. No wonder – if he gave him his coveted poison. After all, they'd need a cover story so no one would get their real connection. They didn't want the whole world to know what was really going on between the two of them. Involuntarily, he looked over to the place where he had sat yesterday.

Suddenly, he grabbed Tom's shoulder.

"Tom, the picture's gone!"

The Inspector looked at him in amazement. "What kind of picture?"

"The one I told you about. Gary Mason's picture with the dedication to Tony. It hung over there yesterday. Now it's gone. Just a space on the wall."

The Inspector nodded. "Yes, now I see what you mean. He didn't even have time to put a new picture up yet." He looked around searching, as if another thought had crossed his mind. "Where's Dickens?"

"He went out half a minute ago," said an officer from the door. "You just said 'morphine.' Then he nodded and walked away. If I'd have known you wanted me to ..."

Tom rushed out into the street. Michael was close behind him.

Ben Dickens was nowhere to be seen. The car of the man who was supposed to shadow him had also disappeared.


Michael dialled the number of the Victor Vorse Dance School. A strange woman's voice answered. "I want to speak to Miss Halliday," he said.

"Unfortunately, that's not possible, I'm afraid," replied the stranger. "Miss Halliday has left us."

"But she didn't say anything about that yesterday!"

"I'm sorry about that," the stranger hesitated. "Do you have a booking?"

"Yes," lied Michael. "For this afternoon. I just wanted to check what time it was for."

"One moment please." He heard paper rustling. Then the voice said, "Can you come at three thirty? You can? Good. We'll see you then."

He was surprised that Vorse let him in. The dance school owner showed no surprise when he arrived. Instead, wordlessly, he led Michael into the studio and handed him over to a slender brunette he addressed as Miss Jackson.

When he was alone with the girl, Michael asked, "Have you heard anything from Miss Halliday at all?"

"No. I only know what Mr Vorse told me. She suddenly had to leave. A family problem. That's why he called me. I always help them out when I can."

While she went to the record player, Michael thought. It seemed like Connie Halliday was afraid to meet him again. That's probably why she hadn't come to work. The dance lesson brought no surprises. Miss Jackson was a more pleasant teacher than Connie Halliday. But he couldn't get her to talk. At least not about her employer. She evaded all of his questions and he was left thinking that he wasn't sure if she was purposely being evasive or if she really didn't know anything at all.

Without further incident, he drove back to his home.

He boiled a kettle for coffee and called Tom Parker. The Inspector was surprised when he heard about the latest development.

"So she has gone to ground, has she?" he said. "And Vorse didn't bat an eyelid when he saw you? Maybe we did him an injustice in suspecting him."

As soon as Michael had hung up, the phone rang. He answered it. "Collins."

"This is Connie Halliday speaking," said a woman's voice, which he immediately recognised.

"Oh, am I pleased to hear from you," he replied sarcastically. "What can I do for you?"

"Listen," she hastily continued. "I don't have time to talk now. Come to Piccadilly Tube Station tomorrow morning at eleven o'clock. The main entrance. Come alone and don't tell anyone about it. I'm relying on you. See you then!"

"Hello, wait!" he shouted. But there was no answer. She had hung up.

Michael held the phone in his hand and pondered. What did the call mean? Was this a new attempt to get rid of him? Or was there more to it?

He decided to let it rest. After all, he couldn't hang on to Tom's shirt tail and phone him every ten minutes with a new sensation that might not come to anything.

Besides, what could happen to him at Piccadilly Station? Surely no-one would risk shooting him in such a crowded place?

133

If he didn't use the entrance, but came by train from another station, he could reach his destination inconspicuously in a stream of fellow travellers.

Also, it was time he was getting back to work. After all, he also had a job to do...

He hesitated. Should he give up now?

Then, nearby, he saw the disturbing figure of a burly policeman who was trying to control a crowd of people around him.

He waited another five minutes, then a minute more but still Connie Halliday didn't come.

Michael walked a few steps into the station. No one seemed to follow him.

He stopped in front of a row of phone booths. They were all occupied. So much the better. Here it wouldn't be noticeable if he waited. Also, if Connie Halliday didn't come, he could call Tom right away. In the booth in front of him stood a girl. But she wasn't using a phone at all. She stood in front of the small mirror attached to the back wall of the booth – and checking her makeup. Michael could clearly see what she was doing even though she turned her back on him.

He had to smile to himself. These girls! Someone could wait a long time until he got to a phone...

Actually, she should have been finished a long time ago. Why did she linger – wait, there was something wrong. She was just pretending to renew her makeup!

In reality, she was watching in the mirror the people walking past the booth!

Their eyes met. The girl turned around, closed her purse and stepped out of the booth. All with a fast, flowing movement.

A tiny, almost shy smile played around the corners of her mouth. Michael stared at her. He couldn't believe his eyes.

Were his nerves so on edge that – as Tom Parker claimed – he was able to see a ghost?

But this girl was really here. For a moment, Michael was faced with a mystery.

# EPISODE FIVE

Michael was still staring at the girl. There was no doubt about it. He hadn't fallen victim to a mirage.

"Karin! Karin Lund!" he shouted.

With a few steps, Michael was with her. He raised his arms – and let them sink helplessly. "I – I thought..."

"You thought I was dead? Murdered?" The smile disappeared from her face. Only now did he realise how tired she looked. Pale and nervous.

"Then the call..." He shook his head in bewilderment.

"I made the call to you." She looked around anxiously on all sides.

He pulled her into a niche between two shop windows. "Connie Halliday called on your behalf?"

She looked at him in amazement. "Connie Halliday?" She seemed to be thinking. "I don't know her."

He grabbed her by the shoulders and tried to hold her eyes with his gaze.

"Well, let's talk about that later. But what about you? Haven't you read a newspaper? They're all full of reports about your murder. Scotland Yard have been working day and night to find out who murdered you. And you – you're standing here in front of me alive!"

It was hard for him to talk to her like that. He would have liked to have taken her in his arms. She seemed so desirable in her helplessness.

But there was no time for that sort of feeling now. He needed to know what was going on. He had to know the truth behind the terrible secret that had already cost the lives of two people. Gary Mason and – yes, and who?

"Tell me," he asked. "Who was the girl found in the flat in Bayswater Road?"

She turned her head to the side. "We can't talk here," she said nervously. "I'm afraid that someone will recognise me. Can't we go somewhere else?"

"Yes. Of course."

He took her arm. They went up the stairs. Up onto Regent Street where he hailed a taxi. While holding the door open for Karin, he gave the driver his address.

When the cab drove off, Michael closed the glass pane that separated him and Karin from the driver. Then he turned to the Swede.

"The police found the body of a girl who – well, who to all intents and purposes at least looked very much like you. Inspector Parker and I were convinced that you were dead. Even after the reports of the murder appeared, no one came forward to say it wasn't you. Neither you nor the film company nor anyone else. Why not?"

She moved restlessly to the side. "I'll explain that to you later," she said.

"But I don't understand why you let the police think you were dead! That makes no sense! Do you have a good reason for that?"

"Later," she said quietly. "I'll tell you everything. But not now. Not here."

For the rest of the trip, they hardly talked to each other. He sat in his corner of the cab and was busy with his thoughts. Michael doubted for the first time that he was a born crime reporter. A crime reporter who had identified a dead woman and then met her in the underground. Who suspected Victor Vorse and the caretaker Bert Howard but couldn't prove anything against them. "I'm just a beginner at all this," he thought bitterly to himself.

Upstairs in his flat, Michael pointed out a comfortable armchair for the girl. Then he went over to where he kept his drinks. "It's a bit early for a drink. But I think we both need it."

Karin asked for a small gin with vermouth. He poured himself a whisky and soda. Then he turned on the electric fire – there was no fire set in the fireplace yet – and sat down on the sofa.

The girl sipped her drink and looked around the room.

"Go on," Michael finally said. "Tell me! I want to know what this is all about."

"Can I have a cigarette first?"

He handed her a box and pointed out the table lighter.

"Are you sure no one can hear us here?" she asked after lighting her cigarette.

"There's no one else here," he reassured her.

She nodded. "I'm sorry, I may be overcautious. But I'm so terribly worried – I can't stand it anymore. I am a stranger in this country. I don't have anyone to turn to. No one who understands me."

Michael got up and paced up and down with the glass in his hand. "Wouldn't it be better if you told me everything from the beginning? I want to help you, but I have to know what it's all about."

Her eyes became vivid. "You want to help me? Out of pity?"

"No, because I – because I think you're nice. And because I think someone has to take care of you."

She put her glass on the table without leaving Michael's gaze.

"But sit down, please. I'm nervous enough." She smiled weakly and waited for him to sit.

"I pace around my room all the time trying to think. To try to think what to do. Trying to find a way out."

"In your room?" he interrupted her. "But I thought you weren't in your hotel anymore? If you were that would have become known immediately!"

"No, I'm not in the hotel anymore. Not since I was murdered, as you believed. I got myself a furnished room on Canterbury Road in St. John's Wood. I've barely left that since. Not since the shooting anyway."

"Because Gary Mason was dead? That's why you could disappear without the film folding?"

"The film couldn't go on, not without its lead actor. I was no longer needed in the studio. It didn't hurt anyone when I disappeared, as you call it."

"And since then you have lived on Canterbury Road?"

"Yes. In front of my window is a small church. I think I know every slate on its roof. I always just looked out and thought about what to do. I've been so desperate."

She stubbed out her cigarette in the ashtray and automatically reached for another one. Michael gave her a light and waited patiently until she picked up the thread of her story again.

"First you have to know who the dead girl is," she said with a little shudder. "Her name was Birgit – and she was my sister."

"Your sister! That's why..."

"Hence the similarity, yes. People have often confused us." Karin Lund sighed. "She was my sister – and at the same time my problem child, you might say. She was a year younger than me, and I always had to take care of her. Our mother died when we were little. Maybe I did everything wrong. I started making films very young. I always had money. Birgit wanted to imitate me, she also wanted to get into the film business. I asked around for her. I tried to generate some interest in her. But she looked too similar to me. The film people just said: We don't need a second Karin

Lund. They wouldn't let me out of my contract so Birgit didn't get in. She must have thought I was jealous of her and deliberately blocked her way. In any case, there was a row. She left and came to England. That was two years ago."

She looked at the smoke rising from her cigarette. Michael didn't make any movement so as not to distract her in what she was saying.

"I don't know how Birgit fared here in London," she continued. "She never wrote to me. As far as I could find out later, she tried to get into the film business here. She obviously didn't succeed. I don't know why. She wasn't untalented, as far as one can judge with your own sister. Maybe she turned to the wrong people. That was possible with her, unfortunately. She has always fallen for anyone who came to her with beautiful words and empty promises."

Michael looked at her. He saw how fragile she looked in the large armchair. How young she was – and how helpless she was in the face of the terrible things she was exposed to in the film industry. Tenderness filled him.

Karin seemed to see through him. Their eyes were on a distant point, on a point that didn't exist.

"Afterwards, Birgit became an air stewardess," she said. "That's when I heard from her again. Acquaintances of ours had flown on her plane and had recognised her. They made an appointment with her in London, but she didn't turn up. They then inquired about her. It could be that she was sick. But they hadn't heard anything. Except for a few strange hints that someone made to them."

Now the girl looked firmly at Michael. Straight into his eyes.

"I was afraid for Birgit," she said. "Everything that people told me when they came back to Sweden seemed so scary to me. That's why I hired a detective agency. I asked them to carefully inquire about her and let me know. Maybe I could help her."

Michael gave her another gin and vermouth. She nodded gratefully, took a sip, and continued: "The news I received was disturbing. Birgit was in – how can I say this – in bad company. Not exactly criminals, but people that spent an awful lot of money in nightclubs but you couldn't find out how they earned it. And she herself also spent more money than she earned at the airline. Much more! She wore expensive model clothes, real jewellery and a mink coat that alone was worth six months' salary. No," she raised her hand defensively, "I understand your gaze, Mr Collins, but it wasn't that. Birgit didn't have a millionaire boyfriend who gave her these things. I would know that. The detectives were very thorough. Nor did she "earn" the money through occasional acquaintances with men – you see, I even thought of that. A stewardess is usually on the road, and then she is, so to speak, under the supervision of her colleagues. In addition she couldn't have been doing that sort of thing without one or other of her work friends being suspicious. Also: I saw a bank statement of hers. Don't ask me how I got it. But believe me, she had an incredibly high sum in it."

"What will become of the money?"

"I don't know. I don't want it. I – I am convinced that it was not acquired in an honest way," she said quietly.

"Blackmail?"

Karin shook her head. "That's what the owner of the private detective agency thought at first. He wrote to me. Under a thousand seals of secrecy, of course. I asked him to investigate by all the means open to him. I then wanted to face her with the information and get her to explain everything to me face to face. Tell her that whatever was going on had to stop."

Her fingers drummed excitedly on the backrest of the armchair. Michael felt all the pain and anguish of the last few months bubbling up inside her.

"But it wasn't that," she suddenly said harshly. "Not blackmail."

"Then what?"

"Drugs."

She looked at him as closely as if she had to study his reaction to what she had said. As if something depended on his judgment.

Michael drew an indifferent face.

"Do you have any evidence of that?" he asked objectively.

She hesitated.

"You mean: Evidence that can be grasped with your hands?"

"That you can show," he said.

"I don't have that. Except for half a confession from Birgit. It was like this: My detective called me. Two of Birgit's colleagues had been arrested. They had smuggled drugs. Stewardesses can do this because they are not searched by customs anywhere. The two stood out because they spent a lot of money. They were monitored and caught. Dismissed on the spot and immediately sent to prison. My detective learned that a third stewardess had also been under suspicion. They just couldn't prove anything against her. But she was monitored – Birgit, my sister!"

"And what did you do?"

"I had just made a movie and was thinking about what to do next. I had several offers. This one from London, was the worst. I accepted it immediately, even though my agent was furious with me for doing so."

"Here in London, you went to see your sister?"

"Yes. I was lucky. She was at home. Alone..."

"What did she say when you suddenly appeared?"

"At first I had the impression that she was happy. But then I told her why I came. She yelled at me and attacked me like a hell cat – she was furious with me. I struggled to fend her off."

"And then?"

"Then all of a sudden she collapsed and cried. So much so that I could hardly understand what she was saying. She no longer denied about the drugs. But she didn't admit it either. She was very upset and I didn't want to push her too hard. I'm not a judge. I just wanted to help her."

She was silent.

Michael didn't let the girl out of his sight. Thoughtfully, he asked, "Have you been able to help her?"

"At first I thought so: yes. She promised me that she wouldn't do anything like that anymore."

"Wasn't that – I mean, could you believe her?"

"Definitely. The fact that she had already been monitored had frightened her tremendously. She even quit her job at the airline of her own initiative. I was there when she wrote the letter and posted it. She was certainly serious about it."

"What happened then?"

"The next evening I was with her again. A phone call came. I couldn't hear everything. The phone was in the next room. But I understood the gist of what was being said: the caller wanted to persuade her to continue."

"And your sister?"

"She coolly refused. She was cool and superior. I already said that she had acting skills. In reality though, she was not in control of the situation. When she came back in the room, she trembled with fear."

"Because of the person who'd called her?"

"Yes. She must have been terribly afraid of him."

Michael smiled imperceptibly. "Unfortunately, this fear was only too justified. Did she give any indication of who the caller might have been?"

"None. I asked, of course. But she just clenched her mouth. Very tightly. I then suggested to her that she move in with me at the hotel. We agreed that she should not leave it on her own. When I finished filming, she was going to come back to Sweden with me. Everything she had was moved to the hotel so she had no reason to leave it. She had the room next to mine."

"But then she did leave it?"

"Unfortunately. I don't know what prompted her to do so. I came back from the studio around six o'clock. She was not in the bar or in the restaurant. I knocked on her room door, but she wasn't there either. Then I asked the doorman. He said she had taken a taxi."

"Well, thank God at least a clue!"

"What do you mean?" She looked at Michael questioningly.

"Maybe we'll find the driver," he told her. "Then we could find out where he dropped her off."

"But in the newspaper report it said that I – that you still believed that I was the dead one – I had been seen in a theatre bar a few hours before the murder?"

"Yes – and by me! I was stunned because you ignored me."

"Did that annoy you a lot?"

"Yes. But that doesn't matter now. Anyway, your sister was in the theatre with a man named Victor Vorse. Unfortunately, he denies it, and I don't have any witnesses."

"But the police?"

"They don't really believe me."

"Although the Inspector – I remember him, he was very polite – is your friend?"

144

Michael lifted his shoulders. "He's a professional. I'm an amateur. Maybe he's right. But I don't believe it. It all fits together too well. By the way, have you ever heard the name Victor Vorse?"

"No."

His next question came like a shot: "So why does your Miss Halliday work for him?"

She looked at him in amazement. "You mentioned the name earlier. I can only repeat: I don't know Miss Halliday."

"But she called me yesterday on your behalf."

"Miss Halliday? What does she look like?"

"In her mid-thirties approximately, dark-haired. – Sorry, that's the phone."

He went to his desk and picked up the receiver.

"Mr Collins?" asked an energetic male voice. "This is Sergeant Bloomsbury. I am calling on behalf of Inspector Parker. He'll be waiting for you in ten minutes in front of the post office in Sloane Square."

"What's going on? Has something happened?"

"Someone's been shot. I don't know any details. But the Inspector wants you to come immediately."

"OK. I'll leave right away. Thank you, Sergeant."

"Thank you, sir."

Michael hung up and went back quickly to Karin

"Miss Lund," he said hastily. "I have to leave for a little while. That call was from the Yard. They want me for something. Please wait here for me. There are drinks. The fridge outside is full of food. Please, help yourself to anything you want. But please don't answer the door. Don't open it no matter who's outside. Do you understand me?"

She looked at him from wide eyes. "I will stay here. But you'll hurry? You'll be quick?"

He promised he would and ran to the door. He locked it behind him and raced down the stairs.

Nine minutes later, Michael Collins stopped his car in front of the post office.

Tom Parker was nowhere to be seen.

Michael drove around the square three times and looked in all the side streets.

Nothing. Not even an ordinary policeman was to be seen.

Had something happened to Tom? If someone has been shot there surely would still be a lot going on about the place. He found the nearest phone box, went in and dialled Scotland Yard's number. He was immediately connected to Parker's office. To his surprise, he got straight through to his friend.

"Tom, what is it?" asked Michael. "Why aren't you here in Sloane Square?"

Tom Parker's voice sounded stunned. "Why should I be in Sloane Square?"

"But a sergeant, his name was Bloomsbury, called me on your behalf!"

"Where? At the paper?"

"No. At home. I was talking to Karin Lund."

"What?" exclaimed the Inspector. "With Karin Lund? Are you mad?"

"Of course I'm not."

"Then tell me what you're talking about."

"She got in touch with me this morning! Yes! I know, I know what you're thinking! But she's alive! Believe me. The dead woman was her sister. I can't explain it all to you now. Anyway, I was talking with her in my flat when the phone rang. The sergeant said you were waiting for me here."

"Now look here!" Tom Parker spoke excitedly. Michael's agitation had spread to him. "I don't know any Sergeant Bloomsbury. I also didn't ask you to go to Sloane Square. This must be some kind of hoax. Someone wanted to lure you away from your flat. Who knew Karin Lund was with you?"

"Connie Halliday could have known. And Victor Vorse. I suppose."

"What do they have to do with Miss Lund?"

"I'll explain it all to you later. I have to get back to Karin. Send a patrol car round, can you? OK?"

"OK. It'll be there in five minutes, and I'll come myself. And – listen, Michael ..."

"Yes? What is it?"

"Wait until my men are there. This man is dangerous!"

Michael hung up and jumped back into his car. He raced over the next set of traffic lights at red, was trapped between two trucks for a while until he was able to overtake the one in front of him and then had a clear road to his front door. He didn't wait for the lift. He raced up the stairs taking them three at a time. Always three stairs at a time. Panting, he arrived at his flat door. What did Tom say? That he should wait?

A reasonable bit of advice if the murderer was inside.

But what about Karin!

He pushed the key into the lock. Turned it around. Once, twice. With a push, the door opened.

With one step Michael was inside. He quickly stepped to the side so as to be out of the line of any gunshot.

But no one fired.

No noise came from the living room.

"Karin!" he called out.

There was no reply.

"Miss Lund! It's me, Michael Collins!"

Nothing. The tension was unbearable. He crept to the living room door. It was just slightly ajar. With a jerk, he pushed it open. There was nothing to see. Behind him, the doorbell rang. He turned around. That must be the police. With two steps he was at the door and pressed the button to open the outside door and let them in the building. Downstairs the front door opened. Hurried steps came up the stairs.

He left the flat door open and walked back into the room where Karin Lund had been sitting.

He had been correct. It was empty.

To the right of the window, the curtain moved. It was just the wind. The window was open.

Michael didn't need to look.

It was the window that led on to the fire escape.

# EPISODE SIX

Karin Lund had disappeared. Only the tart scent of her perfume still lingered in the room, and the rest of her cigarette burned smouldering in the ashtray. The draught from the open window tore apart the plume of smoke that rose from it. The window! With four or five quick steps, Michael was there, pulled the curtain aside and leant out. In front of him the fire escape, the courtyard, the back of the houses opposite – but nothing else.

"Mr Collins!"

He turned around. In the door were the two officers from the patrol car that Tom Parker had sent.

"Are you all right?" asked one.

"Nothing's all right," Michael said bitterly. "A girl has been kidnapped. Please don't touch anything until Inspector Parker gets here."

He lit a cigarette and nervously paced up and down. Soon after Tom arrived.

"The flat was empty when I came in," Michael said after a hasty greeting. "The window here was open." He showed Tom the fire escape and then took him across to the table. "This cigarette was almost out. You can clearly see the lipstick on the tip. The ashes are still intact. Karin must have just lit the cigarette, then ..."

"... was kidnapped," Parker added. He went to the open window again and looked at it closely. "No, my friend," he said. "This window hasn't been opened by force. Your guest most likely opened it herself."

"I can't imagine her doing that," Michael disagreed. "But if she wanted air why didn't she open the other window? She could easily have done that. To get to this window, she first had to walk around the desk. But then: Wouldn't it be a great coincidence if she had just opened this window outside of which the fire escape begins? And an even greater coincidence if her kidnapper, as I suspect, just happened to be waiting on the fire escape? It doesn't make sense."

"You're right. Was the flat door locked when you arrived?"

"Yes, twice. It was how I'd locked it myself when I left."

"Well, we can't get any further with that. Can I use your phone?" He didn't wait for the answer, but dialled Scotland Yard. He spoke for several minutes with someone he addressed as "Sir John." Michael didn't listen. He thought only of Karin.

Tom put a hand on his shoulder. "I'm done," he said. "One of these men," he nodded to the two officers, "will stay here until some more men arrive. Then they'll go over this place with a fine-tooth comb. I have to go back to the Yard. You come along and tell me everything you know on the way."

"But what about Karin?" asked Michael on the stairs.

"We're looking for her. The description is on its way to every division. In addition, your entire block will be searched. If someone has climbed down or up that fire escape, they must have been seen."

They got into the Inspector's car. Tom started the engine and drove off.

"So, now tell me."

Michael told him about Connie Halliday's call, how she had asked him to meet her at Piccadilly Station. Of his joyful shock when he'd seen Karin Lund, who was believed to be dead, instead of the dance teacher. About Karin's sister Birgit, who had been smuggling drugs. Who wanted to stop and therefore had to be eliminated. Of Karin's helplessness.

"Come on, now let's not get over emotional about all this," Tom interrupted him harshly. "So, Miss Halliday invited you to a rendezvous with Miss Lund – but Miss Lund claims that she doesn't know Connie Halliday. Can you make any rhyme or reason about that?"

Michael thought. "Maybe," he said hesitantly. "Karin said she hadn't called me. So who did? She didn't know anyone – except the detective agency that worked for her. So I suppose Miss Halliday could be working for that agency. A private detective who's working on Karin's case without actually personally knowing her. That would also explain why she was with Vorse. To shadow him."

"That could well explain it," the Inspector scoffed, turning past a saluting officer into the car park of Scotland Yard, "which is why she lured you into the trap on Melkin Street. But come on, we don't have time to sit here and come up with theories."

Upstairs in his office, the Inspector tore open the door to an outer office where two girls and two men were sitting.

"Hello everyone. This is Michael Collins. He is just as hungry and thirsty as I am. Maggie – a pot of tea and a few sandwiches, please. And be quick about it."

One of the girls got up and disappeared through a side door.

"The rest of you please listen," Parker continued. "Does anyone do shorthand? Good. Firstly, I need the name of the airline that until a few days ago employed an air stewardess named Birgit Lund, a Swedish national living in London. Secondly, I want someone to go through the file of approved private detectives. I need details of a Connie Halliday. Thirdly, survey all private detective agencies: Who's been working for the Swedish actress Karin Lund? Right, now we can go back to my office, Michael."

The tea and sandwiches were brought five minutes later. They hadn't eaten their first sandwich when the phone rang.

Tom answered it. "Yes?" He listened for a few seconds. Then he said: "All the more important then that we find out the name of the detective agency. Make it as fast as you can. Even faster!" He hung up the phone and looked at Michael.

"There is no private investigator in London called Connie Halliday," he said. "Too bad for your beautiful theory. I would have liked..."

The phone rang again. "Yes? Oh, that will please the boss. Thank you very much for letting me know," he said sarcastically.

Parker cleared the line and dialled a number. "Sir John? You remember Tony Argento, the restaurant owner? The one who was injured in the attack yesterday? Michael Collins and I were there. Yes, it does. He has discharged himself from hospital. Just bolted it seems. During the lunch break. His injuries weren't so bad, the doctor says. And the shock seems to have passed off quickly. Quite my opinion, sir. A miserable mess. Of course, we're looking for him already. Yes, the narcotics department is already onto it."

He pressed a red button and dictated the name and personal description of the owner of the Osteria to the sergeant rushing in. "Special characteristics: fresh wounds on the legs. And have the Osteria monitored! Maybe he thinks we didn't find the morphine and has gone back there."

Michael put his cup on the table. "Is he our next suspect?" he asked.

The Inspector shook his head. "No, after all, we were suspicious about him already. But he's the next bankruptcy, you might say. Halliday – there's no information about her. Lund – disappeared. Argento – disappeared. Its... Wait a minute!" Again, the phone rang.

"Yes?" said Tom. "Well, put him on." He covered the phone shell with his hand. "Take the other receiver, Michael. We have the airline." He took his hand away from the speech shell. "Yes? You are the HR manager? Detective Inspector Parker of Scotland Yard here. I understand you've got an important piece of information for me."

"Yes, please very much," a tinny voice came back.

"You dismissed two air stewardesses recently, didn't you?" the Inspector asked. "Two ladies who used to bring certain things across the border illegally?"

"Yes, that's right," it clattered back after a short break. "Of course, we did everything we could to keep the matter as quiet as we could. It would not have been good publicity for us. I have to ask you too..."

"Of course," Parker reassured him. "We don't want to damage your company's reputation. I assure you that the press won't know a thing about it." He grinned at Michael. "I'm pleased just to have this information confirmed. There was a third lady under suspicion, I understand?"

"I really don't know about that," an uncertain answer came back, "this case is beyond my jurisdiction..."

"I know all about her," the Inspector shot back. "Birgit Lund is no longer working for you."

"Exactly!" It sounded like a sigh of relief. "I can't have rumours spreading in the world – uh..."

"Getting out, is that what you mean? You don't need to worry. I only want you to help us solve a murder. Miss Lund was stabbed to death."

"What?" the man said back. "I thought the dead woman's name was Karin Lund? Her sister, I assumed. At least that's what it said in the newspapers."

"That's what we thought at first. But it was a mix-up. The dead woman was Birgit Lund."

"Hm, actually that makes more sense," the voice said, "that in Birgit Lund's flat not her sister, but she herself was found."

"Wait, what did you just say? Birgit Lund's flat? On the Bayswater Road?"

"Yes: Bayswater Road, Ronway Mansions. I have her personnel file in front of me here."

"Thank you," the Inspector interrupted, "Thank you, that's a very important piece of information. I have to take care of it immediately. Thank you very much! I'll call you again later. Goodbye!"

Parker got up and walked to the door.

"What are you doing now?" asked Michael.

"To get an arrest warrant for the caretaker of Ronway Mansions," said Tom grimly. "Against the man who allegedly didn't know Birgit Lund. He claimed that the flat belongs to a mysterious Dutchman named Shroeman. No wonder we couldn't find this mysterious Mr Shroeman anywhere, even though we drove the police of two countries crazy looking for him."

One of the girls from the outer office stuck her head round the door.

"Isn't the Inspector there?"

"No. He has just gone out, but he'll be back soon. What is it?"

"A phone call from your flat, Mr. Collins. The door lock wasn't forced open. And the neighbours didn't see anyone on the fire escape."

"Thank you, I'll let the Inspector know. Has there been any progress otherwise?"

"No, unfortunately not yet."

When Tom Parker returned, Michael was busy eating the rest of his sandwich.

"The warrant's done," said the inspector. "I'm ready to go. Are you finished eating?"

Michael nodded.

Tom Parker stepped up to his desk and pulled open a drawer. He took out a shimmering black pistol and checked its magazine. "Full. Now the shoulder holster."

He took off his jacket, stripped the straps and put the gun in the holster under his left armpit. Then he slipped back into the jacket.

"Can you see that?" he asked.

Michael examined him closely. A small bulge, nothing more: "In any case, I wouldn't notice anything. By the way, there was a phone call..." He reported what he had learned.

"So?" said Tom. He wasn't surprised.

The heavy car found its way through the hustle and bustle of traffic that fills the streets of the City of London at lunchtime. Michael Collins and Detective Inspector Parker sat in the back seats. In front of them the wide backs of two Scotland Yard detectives.

"Does your editor know where you are?" asked Tom Parker.

"Roughly," Michael replied. "Arthur Ford, the editor of the *Comet*, himself specifically instructed me to take charge of this story. Two murders, plus drugs and a few attempted murders, appeals to him of course. Stay tuned, he said. But that's not so important now, Tom. I noticed two things..." He had to hold on because the driver turned sharply to the right.

"And they would be?" asked Tom.

"First, the murder at the film studio. We know that shots were fired. We know that movie star Gary Mason fell down dead. At the time, we were both convinced that the shots were not fired at him, but at his young co-star Karin Lund."

"Right," said the Inspector.

"When it turned out that Mason was addicted to drugs, the picture changed. An addict is easily involved in crime. So, the shots could have been for him as well. Thirdly – now comes my thoughts – it would also be possible that the murderer did not want to shoot either Karin or Mason."

"But at you, do you mean?"

"Of course not. At Birgit Lund! We also confused her with her sister. Why shouldn't the murderer have confused the two of them as well?"

Michael spoke with great urgency. "Suppose it was a hired gangster. His client, whoever it may be, has handed him a picture and said: This girl lives in the so-and-so hotel. Wait until she comes out, follow her to a lonely spot and shoot her. He was ready. He waited for her in front of the hotel. Karin came out. He mistook her for her sister. Followed her. At the studio, he caught sight of her alone and – shot at her."

"That would explain why Birgit was later killed: the murderer was after her from the beginning. That's what you mean?"

"Yes, but that's not all!" Michael carried on quickly. "You always talk about the murderer, Tom. Have you ever thought that there could be more than one? Several in fact?"

"You'd be surprised: I've thought about it quite a lot. If only because two different pistols were used for the raids..."

"Not forgetting the dagger and the hand grenade," Michael added. "I know I'm just an amateur at all this detective stuff. You've rubbed that under my nose often enough. But I also know this much: there is no murderer who uses four different weapons in four different situations."

The car stopped in front of the four-storey block of flats on the Bayswater Road. Tom, Michael and one of the detectives got out. The driver remained in the car.

"Keep the engine running and keep an eye on the entrance!" the Inspector ordered.

The three of them walked towards the wide glass door. Michael pressed the door bell. It opened.

They looked around. The small window behind which the caretaker's flat was located was closed. Tom Parker went to the flat door where Howard's name was written.

The sound of the bell could be heard all the way to the hallway.

But there was no reply.

Once again, the Inspector rang the bell. Again without success.

"There's no point in us just ringing the bell and making a noise," Parker said quietly. "Come on, Jones. Try your luck."

The detective looked at the door. He pulled a metal strip out of his pocket and with one wrench made a mess of the door. Seconds later, he'd broken in.

The flat smelled of food. Daylight fell into the corridor through the open kitchen door. On a hook hung a hat and a coat.

"Let's go in!" Parker quietly ordered.

He went ahead. After a few steps, he stopped. Waited until the detective had closed the door behind them. Then he entered the kitchen, Michael close behind him.

The room was empty.

Parker turned around. He pushed his friend aside. Went to the opposite room door. With a jerk, he pushed down the handle and pushed open the door. In front of them was an untidy living room. A shirt over the back of the chair. Socks on the floor. In the corner a crumpled pair of trousers. An ashtray full of cigarette butts. Two glasses. Beer bottles.

"He had a visitor, our friend," whispered Michael.

They kept searching. But the apartment was empty.

"Well, then we need to start searching this place," Parker said. "Jones, you stay at the door and get him when he comes back. But be careful. He's probably armed."

"With a gun?" asked Michael.

"Or a dagger," was the telling answer.

157

While the Inspector was searching the flat, Michael used the phone and called his editor. Arthur Ford's voice was accompanied by the usual rattling of typewriters. "Do you have a story already?" he asked immediately.

"Not yet," Michael replied. "But it's going to be a big one. I guarantee you that."

"Well, keep at it! By the way, Ben was here."

"Ben Dickens?"

"The great mystery man himself! He asked about you. Rummaged in his desk. Then he left again."

"Couldn't you keep him there? Ask him what he's been doing?"

"There wasn't time, I had to go to the boss. An urgent conference. The funny thing was though: Ben hadn't been gone long, when his wife called."

"And?"

"She wanted to know if we'd seen or heard anything from her husband."

"So he still hasn't been home?"

"Seems not. Sorry, I've got to go. Something's come up. Call me when you can and tell me what you've got so far."

"Hey, Michael!" shouted Parker from the kitchen. "Come here and take a look at this!"

He stood in front of an open rubbish bin. "Do you notice anything?"

"A bandage," Michael noted. "Gauze – a gauze bandage – with blood on it. Looks like someone has changed a bandage."

"Just the one?" the Inspector asked.

Michael found a pair of coal tongs and pulled the pads out of the bin.

"No, that looks more like several small bandages. Four or five, I would..." He broke off and straightened up. "Tony!"

"Exactly. From several injuries from the fragmentation of the hand grenade. Tony Argento came here!"

"Then it has to be his trousers lying over there!"

He ran into the living room and was back seconds later. He held up the trousers.

"Here, the holes from the splinters! He's recently been here and changed his clothes. Where do you think Howard might have taken him? Can't be far away."

"Maybe he's still in the block. In an empty flat, perhaps?"

"Of course, Tom! Birgit Lund's flat!"

"Exactly. Do you remember the number?"

"507. Why?"

"The key board!"

They went to the small office from which the window led to the hallway.

"One key is missing," Tom noted, "but the second one is there. So, let's go up. Jones, you stay down here. Don't let anyone out of the building. Come on, Michael!"

The lift stopped on the fifth floor. Quietly they walked along the corridor. Tom stopped in front of number 507. He put an ear to the door. Then he nodded grimly. Michael understood. Someone was in the apartment.

The Inspector drew his gun and released the safety catch. Then he put the key in the lock. The door opened silently. On tiptoe, they crept to the half-open room door.

Parker pushed it open with his foot. With a jump he stood in the room. Michael followed.

In front of them lay a woman. Next to it, a man knelt. "Hands up, Howard!" Parker's voice sounded cutting. The caretaker slowly got up. Held his hands in the air.

"I arrest you for a murder committed on..."

Parker faltered, took a look at the dead woman. At that moment, Howard jumped at him. Parker's shot went wrong. A window splintered. Howard hit him with full force. Hurled himself at Michael. In the melee, the pistol fell to the ground. Michael pushed his foot after it. But he couldn't reach it.

Then Howard had the gun in his hand.

# EPISODE SEVEN

Michael Collins stood by the wall. Ready to jump. But powerless because Howard had Tom's gun in his hand.

Inspector Parker slowly straightened up without letting his eyes off the gun.

"Give it up, man," he said. "You won't get out of here. Drop the gun!"

The caretaker seemed to hesitate. He thought about what he should do. He took a step back to keep a better eye on his opponents. Then his foot hit the woman's motionless body. Howard winced. He wiped the blood on his free hand onto his trousers.

"The blood on your hands won't go away that easily, Howard," Parker said harshly. "Come along and make a full breast of it to us. That's the only thing that can help you now."

"No," shouted the caretaker to him. "Move away! Get away from the door!" He pointed with the gun. "Over to the corner there!"

Their hands held up at shoulder height, Tom and Michael did as they were told.

Howard went to the door. Without releasing his gaze from them, he pulled the cord of the phone out of the wall with his free hand. Then he was gone with a leap. They heard the door slamming outside. Then the key was turned.

Seconds later, Michael threw himself against the door. Nothing happened.

"Come on, let's try it together," he gasped. "Let's go!"

This time the thin wood began to give way. Then another attempt and there was a splintering crash, and with a kick the rest of the door was out. They stopped to collect themselves for a moment then Michael pointed down the stairwell.

"There he is!"

A wild hunt began. They were younger and fitter than the man they were after. Faster. When they were on the third floor, he was only half a flight of stairs ahead of them.

"Be careful!" Michael threw himself aside. Immediately afterwards, a gunshot crashed too high. The bullet hit the wall above them.

"Leave him," Tom hissed. "Jones is down there."

Of course. The policeman on the ground floor. He must have heard that last gun shot.

They followed more cautiously. Ready to take cover at any moment.

Howard took a look back. Then he ran down the last flight of stairs.

"Stop! Hands up!" The command came from the semi-darkness of a corner.

Howard pointed the gun and shot. Blindly. Once. Twice. Then a shot from the police colleague fired back. Jones only shot once.

Michael and Tom jumped forward. At the foot of the stairs they stopped.

Howard took a step towards them. He tried to raise the gun but didn't succeed. Instead he fell backwards. With a dull thud he hit his head on the stone floor.

He didn't feel anything anymore.

"I'm sorry, sir," said the detective, coming out of a dark corner, "I didn't want to shoot to kill. But it was all happening so fast and I'm not sure..."

"You're injured," the Inspector interrupted. "There, on your upper arm you're bleeding."

"It's not too bad." The detective felt the wound. "It's just a flesh wound, I think."

"Come on, I'll take you to the car," Tom said. "Where are you going to?" he called out to Michael.

"She might still be alive," he shouted back as he stormed up the stairs. His breathing was heavy but his legs moved by themselves.

On the fourth floor there were two women.

"What's going on?" one of them asked curiously.

Michael pushed her aside and kept running.

"Karin," he thought. "My dear girl, if that scoundrel has..."

Panting, he walked down the hallway. He pushed the open door, staggered into the room, fell to his knees next to the woman and turned her over. He saw a distorted mouth and two rigid eyes that could no longer see him or anything else.

He carefully lowered the head.

"Connie Halliday," he said quietly.


A few minutes later, Tom Parker came back.

"Is she dead?" he just asked. Michael nodded silently.

"We've tracked down the private detective agency," Tom reported, just to say something. "It's just come over the radio. Staten Investigations. It's an American company. They've got a branch in London. The manager says he assigned his best agent to the Lund case. Julia Wilding. Works under the code name Connie Halliday."

"Worked," said Michael, pointing his head at the motionless body.

"This is Connie? – Oh, and I thought... "

"Yes," Michael confirmed. "And I was almost overwhelmed by the fact that it was Karin Lund too. What's all that noise about out there?"

"People from the other flats. Being nosey. Wanting to know what's going on. I've sent for officers from the nearest station. They'll be here soon and be able to take charge of the situation until the murder squad arrives."

163

Michael slowly turned around. His eyes scanned the foot of the bed. Then he scrambled around, looked under a cupboard and straightened up again shaking his head.

"What are you looking for?" the Inspector asked.

"Did you search Howard?" Michael asked back.

"Fleetingly."

"Did he have a dagger with him?"

"No."

"A folding knife?"

"No, definitely not."

Michael pointed to the dead woman. "She was stabbed to death. But what with?"

The photographer with the murder squad was still at work when a policeman put his helmeted head into the room.

"Inspector Parker?"

"Yes?"

"There's a gentleman outside. Sounds like he's an American. Says he's the head of Staten Investigations."

Parker fetched the American into the room. "Do you know this woman?" he asked.

The private detective leant over the dead body. "It's Julia Wilding," he said seriously. "She was my best employee."

"Thank you very much for coming so quickly. We can go downstairs now."

Michael joined the two of them. In silence, they rode down in the lift. Michael thought Tom would take them to Howard's flat. But the Inspector went out on the road.

"Over there's a café. That'll be empty at this time of day. Will you come and have a cup of tea with us?"

"I'd prefer coffee," replied the American.

The café was almost empty. Tom walked over to a corner table that was as far away from the windows as possible.

Michael thought back to what happened at Tony's Osteria and was not amused by his friend's caution.

"I'll try and keep this as short as I can," said the Inspector as steaming drinks stood in front of them. "You'll have to make a signed statement later on anyway."

"Ask whatever you want," the American said.

"Thank you. We know that Karin Lund approached you from Sweden. With the job of following her sister. Is that right?"

"That's correct."

"And you assigned this job to Miss Wilding."

"Others too. But mainly Julia Wilding."

"You told Karin Lund, who was filming in Sweden at the time, that her sister was moving in dubious circles. What kind of people were they?"

"I don't have all the names in my head."

"Then I want to ask more precisely: Was a certain Victor Vorse among them?"

"Yes."

"Is that why Miss Wilding worked as a dance teacher at Vorse's Dancing School?"

"That's the only reason. I have to say that Julia Wilding worked largely on her own. She usually only informed me a little about what she was doing. But I know that she was suspicious."

"In what way suspicious?"

"That Birgit Lund was smuggling drugs for someone."

"Suspicious – but she hadn't any evidence?"

"None that I know of – and now we'll never know."

Parker looked at the American. "The night Birgit Lund was murdered, someone was following her sister. This someone has made our work extremely difficult."

The American leaned back. He wasn't sure what to say.

165

"I could now say that I don't know anything," he said languishly. Then he continued more quickly: "But that would be a lie. It was like this: The evening before the murder, Julia Wilding went to the hotel. She wanted to protect the Lund sisters. But only Karin was there. Birgit had disappeared. Miss Wilding knew the bars that Birgit Lund usually frequented. The two girls went and looked for Birgit. I don't know where but I gather they went all over town. In any case, they drove to Birgit Lund's empty flat. The one over the road where Julia Wilding has now been murdered. The police were already there. Someone told them that a murder had happened. It must have been some newspaper man, I think. He told them: The film actress Karin Lund had been murdered. It must have been a mighty shock for both of them. Not just about the murder. Also the confusion about the name."

"Why?"

"You see, both were convinced that the murderer was after Birgit Lund. However now the murderer would think – like everyone else – that he had murdered the wrong sister, then Karin would be in grave danger. At least that was Miss Wilding's reasoning. That's why she took her client to safety."

"Why didn't she come to us the next day?"

"As I said, I don't know the details. But Julia Wilding had a plan. She was sure that she would find evidence at Vorse's Dance School about who Birgit Lund's murderer was. "For a few more days I have to stay at the dance school," she told me. Until then, she wanted to keep Karin Lund hidden in order to make the murderer worried. – I know," he raised his hands defensively, "it wasn't right to leave everyone thinking Karin Lund was dead. But if Julia's plan had succeeded, then she would have been the heroine of the day."

"And Staten Investigations would have had one hell of a good advertisement," Parker said angrily.

166

"For sure," the American admitted coldly. "But you must understand, Inspector, with us in the States..."

"Wait," Michael interrupted him. "Before you explain to us why everything is better in America, I have a question: The evening before Miss Wilding called and asked me to come to Melkin Street. Why? And why didn't she come herself?"

"Why she wanted to meet you, I don't know. But why she didn't go, she told me later on the phone: She was the dance teacher late that evening. She was the last to leave and locked up. When she left the school to meet you, she was hit over the head from behind. Whoever did it must have been in a hurry. He just left her lying on the ground. When she came to, she dragged herself back into the school and slept until noon yesterday. Probably suffering from a bit of concussion, I should imagine. When she woke up, she tried to call me but I was out at lunch. So first of all, she went to see her client. Karin Lund was shocked when she heard about the attack. She wanted to go to the police. I have to admit that Miss Wilding could be a bit stubborn sometimes. In any case she managed to persuade Miss Lund to let her hide her for another day at least. She told me all this when she reached me on the phone later in the day. I literally begged her to go to the Yard at once. But she wouldn't let herself be talked into it. "I just need twenty-four more hours to nail him," she just said."

"Who was she talking about?" Parker quickly asked.

The American looked at him incomprehensibly.

"Would she have got him in twenty-four hours?" the Inspector repeated his question.

"I don't know."

"You don't have a clue as to who she might even have meant?"

"No."

"Victor Vorse perhaps?"

"It could have been," the American admitted hesitantly.

"That must be it!" Michael interjected. "It's very simple, Tom: Vorse overheard Connie Halliday talking to me on the phone asking to meet me, knocked her out or rather Miss Wilding and then drove to Melkin Street to get rid of me."

"I wouldn't contradict you," said the American. "But Miss Wilding has been watching Vorse for months. When the first murder happened, she also initially did think he was the one who'd done it."

"And then?"

"She seemed to have a change of mind– and rightly so! Because it turned out – although unfortunately too late for Miss Wilding – that the murderer was that caretaker Howard."

"No he wasn't," said Inspector Parker.

"What?" the American asked. "I saw it for myself over there: you caught him in the act."

"But without a weapon," Parker said calmly.

"Without a weapon? Then how did he ..."

"He didn't. Miss Wilding was stabbed to death. But there wasn't a dagger in the flat when we got there. Not even a pointed kitchen knife."

"He will have thrown it out of the window for sure."

"The windows were closed," Michael said.

"We also searched the grounds outside," Tom added. "And the staircase. Even the rubbish bins. There was nothing."

The American stood up. "You probably don't need me anymore in that case."

Inspector Tom Parker slammed the door behind the American after he left.

"You don't like him, do you?" asked Michael Collins.

"Not one bit! How are we supposed to catch criminals when people like him behave so recklessly around us?

Concealing important information from us, hiding witnesses..."

"That wasn't him, it was Julia Wilding."

"But he knew about it. I bet you he knows more than he's telling us right now."

"Tom! We're sitting here and talking as if we have plenty of time. But what about Karin Lund?"

Tom looked at him angrily. "For five hours now you've seen with your own eyes what I'm doing."

"But I can't help thinking that she's in the hands of the murderer."

"If he wanted to murder her, he would have done it right away and not kidnapped her first."

Michael waved at the waitress and paid their bill.

"There's no point in us arguing about it," he said.

"Mike, promise me, you won't take matters into your own hands," Parker asked. Michael looked at him blankly.

"What could I do? Anyway, I have to go into the office to file a report. See you later!"


Michael turned off the car radio.

For the fifth time in two hours he turned into the street where Victor Vorse's Dance School was located.

The fog had become thicker. Two more houses – another one. Then came the building he knew so well.

It was dark. The entrance was no longer lit up. There were no lights on behind the murky windows of the dance studio.

He turned right! Luckily, since the school was on the corner.

A window was lit. On the first floor a shadow moved backwards. Or were there two?

He drove the car around the next corner and parked in the darkest spot he could find. Then he walked back the way he'd come, carefully remaining in the shade of trees and shrubs.

169

The air smelled of smoke. The smoke of the city disappeared with the fog to a dirty, faint haze.

The outlines of a man appeared in the glow of a torch. An old man was walking a small dog on a leash.

Reassured, Michael went on. Only when the outline of the dance school appeared blurred in front of him did he become more cautious.

The window at the back was still bright.

The fence was low. Michael jumped over it and ducked down between the bushes.

His watch hadn't a luminous dial on it. He didn't know how much time had passed. But it must have been midnight by the time the light in the school went out. A little later, he heard the front door slam shut.

Then he heard a car door open. An engine was turned on. It took a few times to get it started though. "It's getting cold," Michael thought. Through the shrubs he saw the illumination of the headlights turned on. Now they started to move away. Slowly the sound of the motor faded away. Michael waited. Ten minutes.

Slowly he straightened up. Water drops fell from the brim of his hat.

He bravely stepped out onto the lawn. The school, which was bright during the day, was now gloomy and threatening in front of him.

He scanned the ground with his foot before putting it down. Sure, someone had left. It might even have been Vorse. But if his thoughts were right, then the school couldn't be empty.

His outstretched hand felt for the wall. The plaster was cold and rough. He felt his way along. Above him was the window of the ground floor. At head height. The basement windows below were barred. He felt the iron bars. He moved further along to the next window. The same. He moved farther along ...

Then he reached into a void. He stood as if frozen, but he understood what it was: the door to the garden. The back door of the house. It was open!

Michael hesitated. If the murderer was waiting for him anywhere, it was here. Carefully he pulled his torch out. It was the only weapon he had. A cursed recklessness of him not to even take a stick with him. Slowly he lifted the torch to eye level. Ready to turn it on at any moment. To blind his attacker.

Then he heard a scream! It was Karin!

He was sure it was her voice. A desperate cry.

Without thinking, Michael jumped through the door. He fell over a chair and then picked himself up. He turned on the torch to see where he was going. He found a door into the corridor.

Again he heard her voice. It had to have come out of the basement.

There – the cellar door was open! He turned the torch off! In the dark, he stumbled down the stone steps.

Down there he flashed the torch. It was a dusty corridor with iron doors. He hid behind one of them. He heard rumbling noises behind it.

At that moment, the door was pushed open from the inside. Michael's torch fell to the ground. With both hands he reached into the darkness. He grabbed a shirt collar. The man fought back. Michael fought as hard as he could. He tried to grasp the man's neck. He slammed into the darkness with his other fist. He hit something. A metal object fell to the ground. Then a foot kicked out and threw him back. Michael bounced back towards the wall. He gritted his teeth and straightened up.

Someone was breathing very close to him. Lightningly fast they grabbed Michael. He could feel their anguish, their fright.

And felt the trembling body of a girl.

"Karin!" he whispered.

He heard her gasping for air and put his arm around her protectively. Then the light came on.

In the doorway stood Ben Dickens. He had one hand on the light switch. In the other, a knife.

# EPISODE EIGHT

With her eyes wide open with shock, Karin Lund clung to Michael. Through her coat and jacket, he felt her tremble.

"Dickens," he said, without letting him out of sight. "Ben Dickens. Crime reporter of the *Evening Comet*. My dear colleague. Doing a bit of moonlighting ..."

"Murderer," he wanted to say. He didn't say it.

Dickens didn't listen to him at all. He listened to the corridor. He carelessly lowered his hand that was holding the knife. He still had the other one on the light switch.

"Shall I go for him?" Michael pondered. But something about Ben's attitude made him hesitate.

Dickens turned around. Michael made his way around Karin. He was ready. But Dickens didn't look at him. He looked at the window. The small, gabled basement window under the ceiling.

As if under a compulsion, Michael turned his head and looked upwards. At that moment, the light was extinguished. There was a sound from the door! Michael was in front of Karin with a flash. But the danger didn't come from inside the room.

Over him clanged glass. He saw a shadowy movement at the window. Then a heavy object fell into the basement room and rolled over the stone floor. The same rolling movement. Like in Tony's Osteria. Michael didn't think any further. In a flash, he grabbed Karin by the arm and dragged her out of the room. Did someone shout something in front of him? He didn't pay attention to it. He pulled the door behind her and pushed the girl into the corner of the passageway.

The explosion made the house tremble. Nothing else happened.

"What was that?" Karin whispered into his ear.

"A hand grenade," he replied. She shuddered and pushed herself gently towards him. For a moment he was ready to forget the danger of their situation. But then he reached for her hand. "Come on," he whispered. "We have to try to get out of here."

His foot hit something. He bent down to feel what it was. It was the useless torch. Useless? No, maybe it wasn't.

He gently dragged the girl a few steps behind him, up to the basement stairs. Then he pulled out and threw the torch up with all his might. It made a tiny clattering noise as it landed.

And then nothing. There wasn't any movement up there. Only the bright rectangle of the door stood out very weakly from the dark. So weak that he could suspect rather than feel it.

"Come on," he whispered.

One after the other, they crept up the stairs. Crouched, with tense nerves, ready to face any danger that might lay ahead of them.

But nothing happened. Undisturbed they climbed up. On the top step, Michael stopped and looked out cautiously.

A dim light fell through the small glass window of the dance school door. On the other side, a dark opening: the door to the room that led out into the garden. The way he had come in.

Shouts were heard on the street followed by hasty steps.

Then a shot was fired. Three or four shots from another weapon came back. New calls. Commands. The small glass pane became bright. Someone had switched headlights on outside apparently.

Michael heard footsteps crunching on the gravel path. Then the door opened. A man's figure appeared in it.

The man fired once out into the street. Then he closed the door behind him and stood for a moment in the almost dark hallway, still dazzled by the light on the street. With fast, safe

174

steps, he then walked towards the next door. He passed Michael so closely that the reporter had to suppress his desire to grab him. Then he disappeared into the dark room. He was as silent as a ghost. The carpet dampened the sound of his footsteps.

"Who was that?" Karin whispered behind him.

He couldn't answer. Suddenly at the back of the house it became bright.

"Stop, stop!" someone ordered. A shot rang out. A dull impact was heard somewhere on the wall. Then the man appeared in the room door. A light beam hit him from behind and showed the desperate, rushed movement with which he looked around.

Involuntarily, Michael ducked down in the darkness of the stairwell. Outside, a car drove up. The man in the room door gave himself a jolt. With quick, silent steps he came to the cellar door. Shortly before that, he stopped still and looked around. Michael jumped up and pounced on him.

He was able to grasp his right arm. The side where he held the gun. Then the other threw himself around. The speed and power of the movement overwhelmed Michael. His knee buckled off the back of the man. His grip around his wrist gave up.

Wheezing with effort, he clambered. It didn't help. The hand with the gun came closer and closer. Then a shot rang out. The flash of the bullet scorched his side. Now wasn't the time to worry about that. He reached out again and grabbed the gun with both hands. He forced it to point downwards.

The other man hit him in the face. Michael hardly felt it. The other man also tried now to get back control of the gun and hold it with both hands. They wrestled doggedly. Neither intended to give in.

They were both going to fight until one of them was dead.

Then the other man fell to the ground where he lay still.

Michael wiped the sweat out of his eyes and looked up. He blinked in the bright light. Men were standing in the doorway. He saw uniforms. Police uniforms.

He slowly stood up. A man in a raincoat approached him.

"For goodness sake, Michael. Why do you do these stupid things?" Tom Parker's voice sounded reproachful. "Are you ok?"

"I think I am – yes," said Michael lamely.

"Lucky you. I say, who's that?" Parker knelt down to the man on the floor. Michael bent over him. He saw a face with thick eyebrows and small eyes underneath. A face he didn't know. A soft noise made him turn around.

"What – oh Karin, Miss Lund, I wanted to say. I..."

"Go on calling me Karin," she replied with a smile. "I thought it was nice. Good evening, Inspector."

Parker stood up. "Good evening, Miss Lund," he said. "I can't claim the same right. But I'm happy to see you're still alive," he added seriously.

"Do you recognise this man?" Michael wanted to know.

Tom nodded. "His name is O'Connor. Got a criminal record as long as your arm. Been inside at least ten or twelve times, I should guess. Don't worry about him. You only saved him from life imprisonment."

"But he's still alive," Karin protested. "I have clearly seen him breathing."

"Really?" Tom asked bluntly. "Is the doctor here?"

"Just coming, sir," replied one of the policemen.

"Right, then we'll get out of here and make some room for him to do his stuff," Tom ordered. "Come on you two."

"Search the garden," the Inspector ordered his men.

"And the cellar," added Michael.

Tom looked at him attentively. "What about the basement?"

Michael briefly told him what had happened. That he had made up his mind to do something on his own. That he drove to the dance school and waited until everything was dark. How Karin had screamed and how he had gone to her aid. From Ben Dickens, the hand grenade and to the desperate struggle in the dark.

"And then you arrived with a whole squad of men," he concluded.

Tom nodded. "You weren't at home and you weren't at work either. I couldn't think where else you'd be. Wait a minute – yes, doctor? What is it?"

"That man has to go to the hospital immediately," said the doctor, brushing the dust off his knees. "His lung has collapsed. But I think we'll get him through it."

"That's a relief," Karin whispered, pressing Michael's arm.

"That he's not dead?" he asked quietly.

She looked at him with a look he couldn't interpret.

"He's conscious," said the doctor. "But I need to get him into an ambulance right away. I called for one as a precaution when the shooting started."

"You think of everything, Doctor," Tom said. Then he turned to two officers who came back from the garden. "Did you find anything?"

"Nothing, boss," said one. "A lot of footprints on the damp grass. But there's so many of them. Some of them will be our people, of course. Only behind one bush someone stood for quite a long time."

"That was me," Michael declared.

"Oh," said the detective, "That's all I can tell you right now."

"Good. Then check out the basement next," Parker ordered. "I'm going to find somewhere that we can sit down. I think Miss Lund has a lot to tell us..."

"Boss," the excited voice of the detective came from below. "There's another one here."

Michael and Tom walked down the basement stairs. The bare vestibule was bright. A single light bulb burned from the ceiling.

In the light, they saw a man lying at the foot of the stairs. He was lying on his back. From his chest protruded the handle of a knife. "It's gone in straight into his heart," said Michael quietly.

"Yes," Parker confirmed. "This isn't looking good. Who is it? Does anyone know?"

No one answered him.

He stood up. "So: take his fingerprints. Get them straight to the Yard. I want the night shift to check and see if we've got him on file."

Then he turned away and climbed the stairs slowly. Michael followed thoughtfully.

Karin Lund looked at them with big, horrified eyes. It was as if she only now fully understood the danger she had been in. Michael took her arm and steered her into a room on the first floor. He sat down next to her on the couch. The Inspector pushed an armchair towards the low table and offered cigarettes.

"So, Miss Lund," he said when they had lit their cigarettes. "Now tell us about how you..."

"Wait," Michael interrupted him, "She's innocent in all of this, but I want to know something more important. What happened to Tony?"

"Who's Tony?" Karin asked in astonishment.

"The owner of the Osteria, an Italian restaurant," Michael told her. "Actually, his name is Antonio Argento. By the way, you indirectly owe your life to him."

"Me? Why?"

"Inspector Parker and I were with him when a hand grenade was thrown into the Osteria. It crashed into the bar and rolled towards us. It was the same noise as we heard in the cellar."

"That's why you recognised it and pulled me out of the way?" she asked seriously. "But what about that first grenade?"

"Antonio was injured and taken to hospital. After he'd gone, we found morphine in the restaurant. Gary Mason was a morphine addict. He was a regular of Tony's. The connection was clear: Tony was Gary Mason's supplier."

"Has he been arrested?"

"Not yet. He checked himself out of the hospital. That's why I'm looking for him."

"He's gone back there," said Tom Parker.

"Where?" Michael asked.

"To the hospital. Today about six p.m. he checked himself back in. He even apologised for having left in the first place. Said he had something to do – something he couldn't postpone or ask someone else to do for him. I also know something: He'd been to the Osteria. To see if the drugs were still there."

"Of course they were gone?"

"On the contrary, they were still there. However, there was only distilled water in the ampoules. We decided to make a small change."

Michael grinned. "Good idea. And then what?"

"Then he probably threw the ampoules into the Thames or anywhere else and fled back to the hospital. We immediately arrested him and transferred him to a private room where he'll be taken good care of with a man posted on his door and bars on the windows."

"How might he have known Howard?" Michael asked.

The Inspector lifted his shoulders. "I don't know. But after all, Howard wasn't an honourable man, and criminals get to know each other. I'd much rather know why Howard yelled at us and practically committed suicide. When it's pretty obvious he didn't murder Julia Wilding at all. Is something the matter, Miss Lund?"

Karin was dead pale, her lips trembling. "Julia Wilding is dead?" she asked tonelessly.

"Yes," Michael said seriously. "She was stabbed to death at lunchtime today. In your sister's old flat."

Tears ran down Karin's face. She swallowed. The men looked at each other not sure what to say or do. They were glad when a detective came in.

"There's nothing left in the basement, sir," he reported. "However – in the one room an explosion must have taken place."

"I already know that," Parker said sarcastically. "This gentleman here celebrated New Year's Eve down there. Anything else?"

"I don't know if you know, sir, but the man that was taken to hospital had an American Smith & Wesson pistol in his pocket."

Parker leaned forward tensely. "And the other?"

"The one in the basement? How do you know that he had a..."

"What kind of pistol?"

"A German moult, sir."

"O.K." Tom leaned back into his armchair. "Get both guns taken to the Yard immediately. Get the ballistics guy out of bed if necessary. I need to know at once whether the shots that were fired at Gary Mason and Michael Collins were from either of those guns."

Karin Lund dabbed the tears from her eyes with a corner of the tablecloth. "Excuse me, this is silly of me." She tried to smile. "But all of this, the deaths, my sister – and now Julia Wilding..."

"You didn't know that Julia Wilding was called Connie Halliday when she worked here?" Michael asked carefully.

"No, I didn't know that. Otherwise, of course, I would have told you I knew her when you mentioned her name today."

The Inspector stubbed out his cigarette. "Whilst we're at it, Miss Lund, we were interrupted earlier..."

"You want to know how I got here? It's very simple: Julia Wilding brought me here."

"What?" Parker asked bluntly. "Miss Wilding did? At noon today?"

"Yes. She followed me. Secretly. I didn't know anything about it. She wanted to know if I was being persecuted."

"Wait a minute," Michael said. "Miss Wilding didn't meet up with me this morning, even though she had arranged it. You came to Piccadilly on your own. But Miss Wilding followed you?"

"She followed me, yes. She saw that two men were driving behind us in a car. They followed us to your home, Michael. She saw them waiting in front of your house. Then one of them left and made a phone call. From a phone box. The other stayed in front of the house. Can I have a cigarette, please?"

She blew the smoke towards the ceiling. "When you were gone, Michael, the phone rang suddenly. I wasn't sure what to do. Then she called through the door."

"Julia Wilding?"

"Yes, she called. I recognised her voice and opened the door and let her in. She asked if you had received a call. I told her everything.'"

"What did she say to that?"

"It was as she thought. She told me about the two men in front of the house. She was sure that the two of them had lured you away and were about to come for me. I believed her. We listened at the door. Then quiet footsteps came up the stairs..."

"Boss?"

"What, sergeant?" Tom Parker asked reluctantly.

"Answer from the Yard. About the fingerprints. We've got the man in the basement on file. His name was Joe Smith, done twice for stabbing, once for illegal possession of weapons, and once for the trafficking of foreign poisons."

"Thank you. That's it?"

"At the moment, yes. We rang the ballistics expert and got him out of bed. He didn't swear too badly. He's on his way to the Yard now."

"Good."

The Inspector turned to Karin again. "So, someone came up the stairs?"

"Two men. They stopped in front of the door. We heard them whispering. Then a key went into the lock. We crept into the living room as quietly as we could. I was so scared – I lit a cigarette and then put it down and just forgot all about it."

"I found it," confirmed Michael.

"I hope it didn't burn a hole in the table? It occurred to me afterwards that it might."

"It was still in the ashtray," he reassured her with a smile. "But what did you do then?"

"We climbed through the window onto the fire escape and from there down into the courtyard. There was no one there to see us."

Michael threw a glance at Tom. "And then?"

"Then Miss Wilding brought me here. Mr Vorse welcomed me very kindly and gave me the guest room upstairs."

"What did she tell him?" Michael asked excitedly. "I mean, what reason did she give him?"

"For why she brought me here? Easy. She has..."

"Inspector?" It was the doctor. "Can I have a moment please? I'm done with here. But I noticed something..."

"What's that, doctor? Please, take a seat."

"No, thank you. I've got to make tracks. It's been a long day. So, what I wanted to say: We have three stabbed people in this case so far. I've seen them all. Three stabs in the heart – oh, pardon," he stopped himself, as Karin made a sudden movement. "I'm sorry if I'm upsetting you ... So, I wanted to say: Not only are the length of the wounds similar, also the weapon – it seems to me – they look to be the same in all three cases. I'll have to compare my notes again, but I don't think I'm wrong. Does that tell you anything?"

"That tells me a lot. Thank you very much, doctor, and good night."

When the doctor left, Parker said to Karin, "Now we will be able to finish your account of what happened. So Mr Vorse took you in kindly and Miss Wilding... Wait, what did he call her? Did he say Miss Halliday or Miss Wilding to her?"

"He called her Julia and she called him Victor."

"That can't be – but of course, if you say it..."

The Inspector seemed completely confused. Michael asked the next question. "What reason did Miss Wilding give him for bringing you here?"

"As I was about to say when the doctor came, she told Mr. Vorse the truth. About the two men in front of your house and that we have fled here. Everything."

"And what did he say?"

"He was annoyed," said the Swede. "I didn't understand all the words, but the tone was clear. Then they argued."

"Because of you?"

"No. She wanted to leave. I don't know where to go. He didn't want to let her go. I was in another room, but I was not happy when he said it was too dangerous for her. But then she went anyway."

"Unfortunately. But then what happened?"

"I stayed upstairs in the room I had been given. The whole day there was music in the house. It's a dance school. In the evening it became quiet. Later, Mr. Vorse knocked and said he had to leave at once."

"Where was he going to?"

"He didn't say that."

"What sort of mood was he in?" the Inspector asked.

"He was very excited. He could not keep his hands still and spoke very hastily. I think he was worried about Miss Wilding."

Karin stopped and looked at the door as it opened.

"Sergeant?" Parker asked.

"The photographer and the forensic team, sir. They're finished downstairs. Just this room to do..."

The Inspector stood up. "Then we'll have to go and let them get on with it. Is it all right if we go upstairs to your room, Miss Lund?"

"Aren't there also going to be traces in there?" she asked.

"You're right, of course. What other rooms are upstairs?"

"Next to my room is the office."

"Well, that's where we'll go then."

They climbed the stairs. At the top, the Inspector remained standing and waited for Karin.

"Where is the office?" he asked.

"On the left, the first door."

Michael went first. Suddenly, he stopped. "There's already someone in there, Tom."

The tap, tap, tap of a typewriter could be heard.

"Maybe someone's doing a check to see if the typewriter works," Parker said. "Let's see."

He opened the door and they went in.

The man at the typewriter sat with his back to the door. He slowly turned around. It was Ben Dickens.

# EPISODE NINE

They stood in the open door. In front was Inspector Parker, behind him Karin Lund and Michael Collins. In front of them, at the typewriter, sat Ben Dickens.

"Hello, come in!" he said and stood up. "Good evening, Michael, good evening, Inspector. Would you please introduce me to the beautiful Miss Lund?"

Tom gasped. Before he could say anything, Michael put his hand on the Inspector's shoulder and pushed past him. "Karin, this is Ben Dickens. Chief crime reporter for the *Evening Comet*. The man I'm standing in for at the moment."

The Inspector was still at the door. "He's afraid that Ben will get past us," Michael thought.

"Sit down, Tom," he said. "Ben can't escape us now." He pushed him a chair. Tom sat down without letting Ben Dickens out of his sight. Seconds later, he jumped up. "What's all that racket downstairs?"

He went out. They heard him walking down the stairs. Voices grew louder. Someone shouting very loudly. Then they heard the sergeant say, "He sneaked around outside."

"I'm sorry, I did my best..." shouted the other. The rest of what he said was lost in an excited tangle of voices. Then they heard steps approaching. "After you," said the Inspector outside the door.

Victor Vorse stood in the doorway. His hair hung tangled in his face. His tie was loose.

He greeted Karin Lund, nodded to the two men and then sat down on the edge of the desk.

Outside the door, Tom Parker gave instructions to the sergeant in a low voice. Michael got up and went to him. He took him by the arm and pulled him to the side. "Tom, someone is still missing."

Parker looked at him inquisitively.

"Tony's not here," Michael continued. "Can you have him brought here? He's an important witness, I think."

"But I don't understand..."

"I can't go into it all now," Michael interrupted. "But we've known each other long enough. Believe me my friend: It is necessary. To catch the murderer."

Ben Dickens was the only one who obviously seemed to feel comfortable. He calmly returned Michael's gaze. The others, even the Inspector, seem to be uncomfortable with what was going on.

"Miss Lund," Vorse said hoarsely. "If you were to go into the cupboard behind you, there is a bottle of whisky. There are also some glasses there. Do you mind? If someone wants ice, then you need to get it out of the fridge downstairs. I would do it myself, but I'm obviously not allowed to leave the room."

Karin fetched some ice and poured them all drinks. She tried to smile in a friendly fashion. Nevertheless, the atmosphere in the room was tense.

Vorse raised his glass. They looked at each other in silence and drank. As they put down their glasses, there was a knock. The sergeant stuck his neck round the door.

"Inspector, I have the ballistics expert on the phone. He says it's the same calibre gun as at the other shootings. Most likely the same weapon. He wants to know if that's enough for you or whether he should keep going?"

"Thank you, tell him that's enough for tonight," Parker said. "He can do the other tests in the morning."

When the door had closed behind the sergeant, Michael took to the floor. "When we were interrupted before, Miss Lund was in the process of telling us what had happened in this building today. I think we should hear her account about the end of the day. Karin, you had told us that Mr Vorse said goodbye to you. You heard the front door downstairs close and him walking to his car and drive away. What happened then?"

Karin Lund brushed the hair from her face. "I was sitting in the dark," she said. "Mr Vorse and I had arranged that. So that nobody would think that I was here. Then I heard a noise."

"From outside?" Michael asked tensely.

"No, in the house. I was afraid. I wanted to turn on the light. But it didn't work."

"The main fuse will have been turned off," Inspector Parker suspected.

"Then someone was at the door," said Karin. Her voice trembled. "I didn't know what to do. I felt the draught when the man came into the room. I wanted to call for help, but I didn't make a sound out of fear. And there was no one else in the house who could hear me."

Michael watched the faces of Victor Vorse and Ben Dickens. "I threw the ashtray at him," Karin continued. "I don't think I hit him. But then I suddenly realised that he couldn't see any better than me. I ran past him and went out of the door. He was behind me. When I was at the bottom of the stairs, I felt his hands on my neck. I screamed and screamed. I managed to get away from him and ran to the first door I could find. It was the door to the basement stairs. I couldn't turn back. I quietly ran down there and hid. I thought he wouldn't find me. Halfway down the stairs I stumbled. He heard it and came after me."

All eyes were fixed on her. Even Ben Dickens seemed curious about what she was going to say next.

"I hid myself away in a corner," she said. "I heard him breathing heavily. Then he was at the door. I think he wanted to turn the light on because he couldn't find me in the dark."

"But the power had been switched off, of course," the Inspector interrupted.

"He had to turn back before he followed Miss Lund into the basement," Michael said. "Please, go on."

"Maybe he wanted to make the light work again," Karin continued. "I don't know. In any case, he collided with the other man at the door. They fought with each other."

"That was you, Michael?" asked Parker.

Michael shook his head. "I don't think so. This was all between the door opening and a light coming on in the basement. Was that before or after the fight between the two men?"

"Before," she said.

"So there were two men with you in the cellar before I arrived?"

"Yes."

Parker leaned forward. "You don't know who the other one was?"

"I don't know who either of them were. It was dark. And Michael's torch broke right away. Then someone grabbed me. I almost died of fright. Until I recognised Michael's voice. Yes, and then suddenly it became light..."

"And I stood in the doorway with a knife in my hand," added Ben Dickens.

"With a knife in your hand. You've already told the Inspector, Michael."

He nodded. "Of course. But I think the last member of our illustrious band is arriving."

In the doorway, heavily supported by two policemen, Tony Argento, the restaurant owner from the Osteria stood. Dickens gave Michael a surprised look. "All due respect," he said quietly.

Michael didn't answer him. He turned to Vorse: "Mr Vorse, do you have a nice, comfortable armchair for our wounded one?"

"Next door," Vorse growled. It was obvious to him that he would rather have his tongue bitten off than say that.

One of the police officers fetched the chair. Tony sank into it. He didn't seem to be at all pleased about being brought there from the hospital.

"I'm going to complain to the Chief Commissioner about you, Inspector," he shouted in an angry voice. "I am a sick man. You can't bring me here when I should be in my sick bed. I'll be informing your superiors about this ..."

"Do you take the whisky with or without soda?" Michael interrupted him calmly.

Tony was so stunned that he replied, "With a lot of soda, please," he said. Then he bit his lips and remained silent. His way out was blocked.

Tom Parker looked over at Michael. He had no idea about what was going on. This "gathering", as his friend had called it, was not his idea. Michael nodded stealthily to him. "You start," he said. "I'll chip in when necessary."

"All right," said the Inspector. "Mr. Vorse: When you left the house today around midnight, did you lock the door behind you?"

"Yes."

"You have a good security lock on the door, don't you?"

"Yes."

Vorse's voice sounded harsh.

"You also locked the door to the garden?"

"Yes."

"How do you explain then," the Inspector said, "that a few minutes after you left, Miss Lund was attacked in her room?

How do you explain that someone was able to get through both doors that you say you locked?"

Vorse looked at him with a pinched face. "Are the doors damaged at all?" he asked. "No? Then," Vorse said, and his voice was strangely uncertain, "then – my God, then someone had a set of door keys." He reached into his pocket. Tom Parker's hand disappeared under his jacket.

But Vorse only pulled out a bundle of keys and threw it on the table. "There. This is mine. There is only one other set."

Then he stood in front of Tony Argento and slammed his fist into his face. Three, maybe four times. Until Inspector Parker took hold of his arm with a firm grip and pushed the wheezing man into the opposite corner of the room.

"Do that again, and I'll handcuff you," he warned.

Parker opened the door. He spoke briefly with the two officers who were stationed outside. One of them went away and came back immediately afterwards with a loop of keys.

Parker walked towards Vorse. "Is this the other set of keys?"

Although Vorse was in the shadows, Michael thought he saw him turn pale.

"Yes, it is," he said with a vengeance.

The Inspector showed the keys to the others. He turned to Tony Argento, who smiled at him with distorted swelling lips. "All right, Tony?"

The restaurant owner shook his head. "No – I'm not good," he said weakly. "I need some air. If I can just go to the window for a moment..."

He slowly got up and took two steps towards the window. His foot got caught in the cord of the floor lamp.

At that moment it happened. Vorse literally jumped forward. At lightning speed, he stood next to the door and switched on the light switch. At the same moment as the standard lamp went out, the ceiling lighting flared up. It illuminated Vorse, who stood with his back to the door, with raised fists ready to fight.

Ben Dickens jumped up from his chair. In his hand he held a polished letter opener. The tip pointed to Argento.

"Not through the window, Tony," he said mockingly.

Michael controlled himself so as not to launch himself onto the restauranteur. Instead, he grabbed Argento by both arms and pushed him back into the armchair.

It all happened so quickly that Tom Parker was completely surprised. Nevertheless, he didn't lose control of the situation. "Thank you, gentlemen," he said drily. "Even if it wasn't necessary. Outside in front of the window are another two police officers. Just like on the other side of this door. Only a complete idiot would try to get out of here."

"Or a murderer," Michael said. "Isn't that so, Argento?"

"You're crazy." The restauranteur jumped up with astonishing dexterity. One step...

He didn't get any further. Michael hit him with the force of all the pent-up tension of the last few days behind it. Half stunned, Argento fell back into the armchair and stared at the men through glassy eyes.

Parker opened the door. "Handcuffs," he ordered, pointing to the restaurant owner. "And stay in here. At the door. Mr Vorse, if you'd be so kind as to go back to where you were standing before."

"So, Michael," said the Inspector, "And now, may I ask you for an explanation."

"With pleasure. Above all, you will want to know how I came up with the idea that Argento is our murderer – the instigator of all this. I only fully understood it here in this room. Suddenly, the pieces came together like a puzzle. But it started much earlier. When was it, Vorse?"

"About a year and a half ago," said Victor Vorse, "when Tony came up with the idea of organising a drug smuggling ring."

"It was his idea to have the stuff brought into the country by air stewardesses?" Michael asked.

"Yes. He knew three who always ate at his restaurant when they were in London. He persuaded them to bring the stuff in. From then on, of course, they weren't allowed to be seen with him or go to his restaurant."

"That's why he was looking for somewhere the girls could go to regularly without it being noticed," Michael noted. "A dance school was ideal for that, wasn't it? The girls passed you the drugs. Who picked them up? Argento himself?"

"One of his people. Either an Irishman, his name's O'Connor, or Smith."

"Smith is dead," Michael said quickly. "The other one has a collapsed lung."

"Then you've smashed up the gang," Vorse said soberly. "That's good."

"But I..."

"Mr. Vorse," the Inspector interrupted, "anything you say here you will have to answer for in court..."

"Thanks for the caution, Inspector." Vorse looked down at his cramped hands. "But nothing matters anymore."

"You will also need him as a key witness," Michael reminded him.

"Of course," Parker admitted. "I'll do my best to see that it doesn't go badly for him. Keep talking, Mr Vorse. One of the stewardesses was Birgit Lund, wasn't she?"

Michael sat down next to Karin and put his arm around her shoulder. Vorse followed him with his eyes.

"Birgit was a magnificent girl," he said. "Sure, she was crazy about money, wanted to make something of herself. She had expensive tastes. She wanted the lot. Furs, jewellery, beautiful dresses. She wanted to get somewhere, be someone. But otherwise she was fine. We often went out together. We had lots of fun together. She had plenty of money and didn't mind spending it. Then came Julia. For me, it was something like love at first sight. Well, and with her too probably. But we didn't admit it to each other until much later. At first I only knew her as dance teacher Connie Halliday. But when it became serious between us, she told me the truth. She told me everything. That her real name was Julia Wilding. That she was a private detective and worked for Birgit's sister. I promised her that I would never have anything to do with drugs again. I kept my promise."

He looked up. "Tony threatened me. I just laughed at him. He couldn't force me to keep doing it. I also warned Birgit. That's why she had no drugs with her when the contact came. Birgit met me afterwards. She didn't want any part of it anymore. But she was afraid of Tony. She waited until her sister arrived in this country. Then she finally told him it was over as far as she was concerned."

"Did you tell Miss Wilding about Tony?" Parker asked.

"No. She guessed it. But I didn't confirm it to her. I wanted her to stay out of all this."

"But she didn't give up anyway?"

"It left her no peace. She loved me. But she also loved her work. And she wanted to help Karin Lund. That couldn't end well. When she didn't come back tonight, I decided I had to do something. I went to Scotland Yard. The man there told me you were out, Inspector. So I waited for you to come back."

"How long did you wait for?"

"For half an hour perhaps. Then I heard two officers talking about a new murder. Of a woman. I drove here immediately. It could only be Miss Lund or – or Julia. When I saw Miss Lund sitting here, I knew that it had to be Julia who was dead. But I didn't want to believe it. But I understood that the gang had Julia's keys."

"Who committed the murders?" Parker asked.

Ben Dickens turned around in his chair. "I can answer that question," he said. "You know that I've been a crime reporter for twenty-five years. That's a long time when you have a good memory – and a good archive. I saw Tony Argento the first time when he was sent to prison eighteen years ago. He had stabbed his girlfriend."

Argento moved in his armchair. Dickens didn't pay any attention to him. "Unfortunately they couldn't prove any intention to murder her. So he got away with a manslaughter charge. When he was free again, he opened the restaurant. I didn't worry about him any further. Until I noticed that there were so many drug addicts frequenting the place. Among them Gary Mason. He was shot – in the presence of Karin Lund. That was a big moment for me, because I knew that Karin's sister Birgit was in contact with Tony, Mason's morphine supplier. The case interested me so much that I took a holiday to focus on it. I have to admit that I had another motive. There was a young man sitting in the editorial office who thought he could be a better crime reporter than me – if only someone would give him a chance. So I thought Michael could cut his teeth on this case."

Michael smiled. "And besides, you wanted to show the loud young man how to solve such a case..."

"That too. Unfortunately, I arrived too late, which is why Gary Mason died. Otherwise, the other murders wouldn't have happened. Tony couldn't any longer lie to Mason because the girls were gone. Mason tried to blackmail him. He wanted his stuff. He knew everything, including about Birgit Lund. He probably threatened to tell Karin Lund who was his co-star in the film."

195

Karin lifted her head from Michael's shoulder. "Oh, that's why he tried to talk to me secretly. I tried to keep my distance from him. He was so scary sometimes. Like there was something wrong with him."

"He was suffering from withdrawal symptoms," Ben said.

"Anyway, Tony kept an eye on him. But when he became dangerous – Bang! Who was it that shot him by the way?"

"The bullets came from Smith's gun," the Inspector said. "But what about Birgit Lund? And Bert Howard? Who killed them?"

"I only realised that today. When I came up with the idea of seeing who owns the flat. Tony Argento was the boss. Howard was in it with him. He kept watch on Birgit, having sold Tony the flat himself. Right, Tony?"

Argento straightened up. "I'm fed-up with all this ridiculous talk," he said hoarsely. "None of it's true. You are all lying. You're making it all up! Birgit Lund..."

"You stabbed her yourself," said Ben quickly.

"This is a lie!" shouted Argento. "Smith and O'Connor did everything on their own."

Dickens looked at him coldly. "And who met with the two of them this afternoon? Who gave them the knife with which he had killed Julia Wilding a few hours earlier? Who gave them the order to stab Karin Lund with this knife while he was lying in the hospital?"

Argento stared at him like a ghost. His swollen lips trembled. Michael understood that Ben Dickens had only bluffed. He did the same thing before Argento could extricate himself.

"Howard has confessed," he said. "He knows you killed Birgit Lund and Julia Wilding. He wants nothing to do with you anymore. The murderer is you, Argento!"

Tony raised his handcuffed hands to his head.

"The cowards have betrayed me," he said hoarsely. Then, suddenly, he said, "Yes, it's true. It's all true. And now get me out of here. Fast."

The Inspector brought in the two police constables. "Take him away!" he ordered.

Then he turned to Dickens. "Had you worked all this out?"

Ben shook his head. "Not quite. I knew a lot. In any case, I heard late this afternoon that Argento was back in town and had seen Smith and O'Connor. Then he checked himself back into hospital so since then I followed the two of them. Until we came here to the house."

"Where you just got here in time to save Karin's life," Michael said.

"Both of us did that," Ben said with a smile. "You and me. You have the gangster..."

"Smith," the Inspector added, "... intercepted at the door." Ben ended his account. "He dropped his knife..."

"Of course," Michael recalled. "I heard something falling. And you picked up the knife?"

"Luckily. Then I turned on the light. You saw me and was finally convinced that I was the murderer. Yes, you ought to feel ashamed. Anyway, then someone was at the top of the window."

"O'Connor," said the Inspector.

"Of course. I thought he called out. That's why I turned on the lights. But he threw a hand grenade. I wanted to warn you, but you were already outside. At the stairs I came across Smith again. That was his bad luck. This time I had the knife."

Parker nodded. "Impeccable self-defence. But the hand grenade in the Osteria? Was that all set up so that we wouldn't suspect Argento was involved in anything?"

"Of course," Michael said. "The grenade was meant to land behind the bar. But instead, it bounced against it and came rolling back."

"That's all clear so far," said the Inspector. "But there are still things I'll want to talk to you about, Mr Vorse. You must of course keep yourself at our disposal..."

He pulled him into a corner and spoke softly to him.

Michael looked at Karin. "I want to know something else," he said. "If you – sorry if you..."

She looked at him with wide eyes, expectantly.

He searched for words.

The tapping of the typewriter interrupted him. "What are you writing, Ben?"

"The report for the *Comet*," Ben said without looking around.

"Aren't you on holiday anymore?"

Ben Dickens turned his chair around and looked at the two young people.

"Unfortunately, I have to end my holiday," he said with playful regret. "As I see it, you are concerned with more important things. In addition to that, just remember I'm the crime correspondent of the *Comet*."

"Was I that bad?" asked Michael.

Ben smirked. "Not that bad. But you're going to have to stick with the movies from now on. I don't think Miss Lund wants a man who runs after criminals – instead of being with her." He turned around and immediately continued to write. Karin was blushing, she'd heard everything Ben had said. "He's right," she said quietly. "You're going to have to stick with the movies."

# END

# COFFEE BREAK

Carl Zeppa Sherman, chief executive producer for the Harrison Film Corporation, wasn't surprised when Superintendent Hamer of Scotland Yard paid a visit to the Harrison studios.

It was twenty-four hours after Sylvia Lincoln had swallowed the fatal dose of arsenic.

Hamer said: "You know why I'm here, Mr Sherman."

Sherman nodded, took the cigar from his mouth, and snapped into the telephone, "Don't disturb me for the next fifteen minutes. I'm all tied up." He looked at Hamer.

The Superintendent said, "Is it your opinion that Miss Lincoln committed suicide?"

Carl Sherman hesitated: he stared at his cigar for a moment, then nodded his head.

Hamer said: "Had anyone in the studio a particular reason for wanting to get rid of Sylvia Lincoln?"

"So, we're looking for the good old-fashioned motive!" exclaimed Sherman with a pained expression. "This is just like a corny situation out of a Hollywood whodunnit!"

"Don't let your sense of humour get the better of you, Mr Sherman. I've got a hunch that someone in this studio played a pretty unfunny trick on Miss Lincoln."

Carl Sherman looked the Superintendent straight in the eye. He said quietly: "Any ideas, Mr Hamer?"

"Suppose we accept the suicide theory for the moment," the Superintendent said. "Have you any idea why she should have committed suicide in the canteen?"

"I haven't the remotest idea," Sherman answered and added with a smile, "Your guess is as good as mine."

The Superintendent said quietly: "My guess is that Miss Lincoln didn't commit suicide."

"But she must have committed suicide!" Sherman laughed. "We all know the coffee's pretty bad in the canteen, but it's not that bad!"

Hamer paused, then said: "I'm going to ask you a very personal question, Mr Sherman."

Sherman stubbed out his cigar in the ashtray. He looked uncomfortable, but his voice was quite steady. "You're the most persistent guy I've met since I've been over here," he said. "However ..."

"Was Sylvia making a nuisance of herself?" Hamer asked.

"You mean here, at the studio?"

"No."

Carl Sherman shook his head. His hand was trembling slightly. "I'm afraid I don't get you."

"It's really quite simple," said Hamer. "I'm asking you whether Sylvia Lincoln was making a nuisance of herself."

"What you're really asking me," Sherman declared, "is whether my private affairs caught up with me and started to interfere with my duties as chief producer for the Harrison Film Corporation?"

"You can put it that way if you like," Hamer replied.

"Whichever way you put it," Sherman said, "I guess it whittles down to the same thing. Did I murder Sylvia Lincoln?"

Hamer said, quite simply: "Did you, Mr Sherman?"

"No, I didn't," said Sherman emphatically. "Though God knows there were times when I was tempted."

Hamer smiled and crossed to the door. "I'll see you later," he said. "I'm going down to the canteen."

As he strolled down the corridor, he could hear Sherman on the telephone. "I can't make it this afternoon," he was saying. "I'm all tied up." He sounded very worried.

Mrs Muriel Cross had been in charge of the canteen at the Harrison Studios for seventeen years. She was a stoutish little woman with a jovial manner and a tongue that never stopped wagging.

When he'd accepted a cup of tea, the Superintendent said: "Now, tell me exactly what happened yesterday afternoon, Mrs Cross."

Mrs Cross said: "Miss Lincoln came into the canteen about half-past four. She was with Charlie West, our dress designer; Beryl Drake, the actress; Tim Lowe, the assistant director, and Mr Sherman. They ordered coffee and sat over there at the corner table." She pointed to a table at the end of the canteen.

Hamer asked: "Who served the coffee?"

"I poured it out myself," Mrs Cross told him, "but Mr Sherman was at the counter buying some cigarettes and he insisted on carrying two of the cups across to the table."

"Did Miss Lincoln strike you as being downhearted about anything?"

"I don't think so, sir. If you ask me, they appeared to be quite a jolly party."

"And what about Mr Sherman?" asked Hamer. "Did he strike you as being particularly jolly?"

"He was pretty much the same as he always is," said Mrs Cross. "Until his stomach started to bother him."

"And then what happened?"

"Well, it was most unusual. He was perfectly all right one minute and the next minute he was howling his blinkin' head off for some magnesia."

"Thank you, Mrs Cross," the Superintendent said quietly. "You've been a great help."

He finished his cup of tea and strolled out of the canteen.

Carl Sherman was on the telephone when Hamer returned to the office. As soon as he saw the Superintendent, he snapped into the mouthpiece: "I can't discuss the schedule any further at the moment. I'm all tied up."

He put down the receiver and smiled.

Hamer said, "I've just had an interesting chat with Tim Lowe. He tells me that shortly before you had your spot of stomach trouble you laboured under the impression that you'd taken a drink from the wrong cup – from Miss Lincoln's cup, in fact."

Sherman looked angry. He said: "What precisely are you getting at?"

"I'm getting at the fact that you knew perfectly well that one of the cups contained arsenic. You thought you'd taken a drink from that cup – that's why you suddenly got frightened and demanded some magnesia."

Hamer paused.

"You know as well as I do," he went on, "*that magnesia is a rough antidote to arsenic poisoning.*"

Sherman opened his mouth, then closed it again. He looked very frightened.

The telephone rang and the Superintendent picked up the receiver.

A curt, crisp voice said: "Listen, Carl! We want you for an executive meeting on the 14th, a personnel meeting on the 17th, and a script conference on the 21st."

Superintendent Hamer said: "I'm sorry, but Mr Sherman won't be able to make it." He added as an afterthought: "He's all tied up."

# THE END

Printed in Great Britain
by Amazon